tadpoles in my jar

This is a work of fiction. Names, characters, places, and incidents are either the product of the author's imagination or used fictitiously. Any resemblance to actual persons, living or dead, events, or locales is purely coincidental.

Cover design by Mary Kathryn Groh
Published in the United States of America

ISBN 979-8-218-70658-6
Second Edition

Published by Mary Kathryn Groh

This book is dedicated to

seventeen-year-old me, who chased sunsets and lightning bugs, who romanticized everything, and who believed that one day, she'd write something that mattered.

You did it.

Track	Title	Date
1	nine years later	June 1997
2	august	August 1997
3	new york city	October 1997
4	autumn	November 1997
5	confetti	November 1997
6	the 3rd of december	December 1997
7	mcgregor's nook	December 1997
8	new year's eve	December 1997
9	to the lighthouse	January 1998
10	the old reynold's house	February 1998
11	the poetry reading	March 1998
12	the treehouse	April 1998
13	for betty	May 1998
14	seventeen	May 1998
15	the fourth of july	July 1998
16	where the lilacs bloom	August 1998
17	Cardigan	August 1998
18	The One	August 1998
19	Ghost	August 1998
20	Cough Syrup	August 1998
21	Something is Very Wrong	August 1998

Prologue

It was the summer they turned seven when James and Betty discovered the magic of the creek. They ran barefoot down the dirt path, with wildflowers and tall grass brushing against their ankles. The trail was lined with monstrous trees, their branches stretched out as if they might reach down and grab them.

When they arrived, they dipped their toes into the cool, rippling water, and everything else seemingly faded away.

James, a lanky boy with untamed brown hair, knelt beside the water, crafting a sailboat from a leaf and a twig. Carefully, he set the boat afloat, and the two of them watched in silence as it drifted downstream, navigating the currents.

Betty picked up a slender stick and poked it into the murky bottom, swirling it. Her eyes lit up as she spotted a tadpole darting past. Grabbing her mason jar, she scooped it into the water, the tiny creature wriggling around inside. She held the jar over her head, her smile as bright as the sun reflecting off the water.

"I got one, James!"

Betty's eyes shifted to the rope hanging from one of the low-hanging branches. She set her mason jar in a pile of leaves and scrambled up the tree's vines and roots. Balancing on her tiptoes, she stretched out, gripping the rope with both hands.

"You won't do it," James teased. "You're too scared."

"Watch me."

With a deep breath, she stepped back, her toes sinking into the dewy grass. As Betty gripped the rope tightly, her hands burning from the coarse fibers, she squeezed her eyes shut and leaped into the air.

Soaring seven feet above the Ohio creek, a high-pitched scream escaped her lungs. Her outstretched legs grazed the grass as she swung back toward the tree. With a relieved sigh, she glanced back at the rope, then turned to James, giving him a playful curtsy.

As the sun dipped lower in the sky, James and Betty made their way up the dirt path, their legs caked with dried mud and their clothes damp. Betty cradled her mason jar while James carried a stick, swinging it at the tall grass. Wild tangles of hair clung to their foreheads, but neither seemed to notice.

"We'll always be best friends, right?" she asked.

James didn't answer at first. Then, he linked his pinky with hers. "Always."

Every so often, they caught each other's eye, their dirt-streaked faces beaming with the kind of joy only summer days like this could bring. James and Betty promised they'd return to their secret kingdom soon, their minds already racing for their next adventure.

Chapter 1
nine years later
Betty

I hear the unmistakable growl of James's truck pulling into the driveway. The rusty tailgate rattles like a loose tooth, no matter how many times he tinkers with it. Then, three short honks; a secret code we've had since the fourth grade when he started picking me up on his bike. Back then, he wore a helmet that was slightly too big for his head, and his handlebars were wrapped in duct tape.

We drive down Oakwood Avenue, the truck bumping over familiar potholes. Mrs. Callahan's hedges reach for the windows, curling over the glass as if to hide the house from prying eyes. Mr. Garver's collection of gnomes is just as ridiculous as ever. And then, I notice something new, something I've never seen before — a moving truck parked in front of the old Reynold's house.

"No way," I mutter, nudging James. "Someone actually bought *that* house?"

James follows my gaze to the paint-chipped, battered home that everyone in town swears is haunted.

"Looks like it," he says with a chuckle. "Think they know about the ghosts in the attic?"

"They'll figure it out soon enough."

We veer off the road, the tires crunching over gravel. The

truck sputters to a stop, kicking up a final puff of dust as the engine dies. We walk down the overgrown trail, where golden rays of sunlight filter through the towering trees, casting long shadows on the path in front of us. The creek hasn't changed at all; the water is clear and cold, rippling over smooth stones.

Without hesitation, we kick off our shoes and plunge our feet into the shallows. The sun-dappled water laps at my legs, sending goosebumps racing up my arms. James wades in beside me, his shoulders relaxed, like this is where he belongs.

It's where we both belong.

He crouches beside the shore, brushing moss off a boulder near the edge. "This one here?" he says, glancing back at me. "I think this is the rock you face-planted on a few years ago."

I laugh, surprised he remembers. "I sprained my ankle so bad I couldn't walk for days."

What I don't say is how I felt in that moment: how James lifted me in his arms, how he made me feel safe in a way I couldn't explain, how I held my breath the entire walk back, trying to make sense of the sudden flutter in my chest. That was the first time I thought of James as something more than my best friend. And now, standing here beside him, I feel it again—stronger this time.

James picks up a flat stone and skips it across the creek. The ripples spread outward, overlapping each other, until they disappear. He glances at me, his eyes lingering on mine for just a second longer than usual, lips twitching like he's about to say something. But he doesn't.

The sun gradually begins descending behind the tree line, painting the sky in deep shades of orange. I tilt my head up to the sky, the bubblegum-pink clouds reminding me of the cotton candy from the Gallia County Fair. When the sun is completely gone, replaced by stars that scatter across the sky like spilled sugar, we take off again. Faster this time.

As the truck barrels down the street, I turn on the radio, letting Journey blare through the speakers.

"Oh, turn it up... I love this song."

I glance at him, surprised. "Since when do you love any song that was made past 1979?"

"Hey, I'm not a complete music snob." A crooked grin tugs at the corner of his lips. Reaching over, he cranks the dial.

Then, we both start singing.

"You're so off-key," I tease, bumping his shoulder.

We keep singing, louder now, harmonizing terribly. His fingers drum along the steering wheel, while I stick my head out of the window, letting the wind whip my copper braids around like wild ribbons. And for a moment, it's like nothing else exists.

Just us. This song.

This truck. This perfect moment.

The song fades into something newer, something neither of

us recognizes. But the silence between us grows louder than any song on the radio.

We pull onto Chestnut Avenue, where James parks his truck between my house and his. The street lies in near darkness, broken only by the faint amber glow of the street lights.

I don't move right away. Neither does he. Seated side by side, our fingers are almost, but not quite, touching. I sit frozen, heart pounding so fiercely I'm certain he can hear it. It's in this stillness that James's voice breaks through, hesitant, yet sure.

"Betty... I—"

Suddenly, his hands reach for my face, his fingers gently brushing my cheeks. They're rough and warm — his hands that once held mine at Grandpa's funeral. And now, they're here, holding me in a way they never have before.

Then, he kisses me.

His lips are softer than I imagined, and when he pulls back, our eyes lock. I'm not sure what to say. All I know is I don't want this moment to end.

"You kissed me," I whisper, breathless.

His lips curve into a nervous smile. "Was that okay?"

I don't answer. Instead, I smile, grabbing his shirt and pulling him back to me.

I lose myself in the kiss for a moment—until a sudden

knock on the window jolts us apart. My heart plummets when I look up to see Dad's silhouette standing outside the truck's window. James fumbles with the window crank, his face draining of color.

Dad steps closer. "What are you kids doing out so late?"

Cheeks burning, I shift uncomfortably in my seat.

"I-it's my fault," James quickly blurts, his voice faltering slightly. "I'll make sure she's home earlier next time, Mr. Thompson. I promise."

"Good," Dad says, fixing a glare on James. "Because if you don't, I've got Sheriff Cohen on speed dial."

James quickly nods.

Dad opens the door, the hinges creaking slightly. "Say goodnight to James."

I slide out, Dad's firm hand resting on my shoulder. As he pulls the door closed behind us, I glance over my shoulder. James smiles, that small, crooked one that always makes my heart flutter.

Dad clears his throat, his grip tightening as he guides me toward the porch. For a moment, I feel like a little kid again, caught, guilty. But even as my stomach twists, my mind drifts back to the feeling of James's lips on mine.

I've had a crush on James for a really long time, but it was always just that — a crush. Like something I'd scribble in my diary, then hide under my bed.

After that night, everything felt different. Neither of us talked about it, but we didn't need to. The way his hand lingered on mine, the way he looked at me like I was the only person in the world, the way his breath hitched ever-so-slightly when I leaned in, it was there, in the quiet moments, slowly unfolding between us.

While my friendship with James began to change, Gallipolis stayed exactly the same: the smell of fresh bread from the bakery on 3rd Street, the clanging of the church bells every Sunday morning, and Dolly, the waitress at Marg's Diner, never without a cigarette dangling from her lips. Gallipolis felt like a place where time stood still.

I didn't know it yet, but that August would change everything.

Chapter 2

august

James

I'm jerked awake by the relentless pounding on the front door. With a groan, I squint at the clock: 8:34 A.M. I lie there for a second, blinking, hoping someone else will answer. The house is quiet. Dad's finishing an overnight shift, and Julie? Who knows.

I sigh and drag myself out of bed, my feet hitting the hardwood floor. The stairs creak beneath my weight as I shuffle down, still half-asleep.

When I open the door, I see Betty standing there. Her cheeks are blotchy, streaked with tears that haven't fully dried. She doesn't say a word, just steps past me. She doesn't even look like herself. For a second, I wonder if I'm still dreaming.

"Can we talk?" she whimpers.

I lead her upstairs, my mind still foggy as I look around at the mess in my room; clothes scattered across the floor, a half-eaten bag of chips on my desk. It's not the most welcoming place, but I clear a spot on the bed and gesture for her to sit. I take a seat next to her, my body stiff, waiting for her to speak. My mind races.

Is this about us? What did I do? Is she upset with me?

She wipes at her eyes, sniffling. And then, in a small voice that cracks, she says, "James, I'm moving."

I blink. "Like to a different house in town?"

Her eyes well up again, and she shakes her head. "To New York City." She stares down at her hands, her fingers tugging at her friendship bracelet. "My dad... he got a job there."

New York. The words don't even make sense coming from her mouth. She belongs here. In Gallipolis. With me.

"When?"

"The end of the month."

We've still got time. That's what I tell myself — like a kid believing in magic. I pull her into a hug, her body trembling against my chest. Her hair smells like lavender, and I try to focus on that instead of the knot forming in my stomach.

She pulls back slightly, her puffy red eyes searching mine. "Everything is going to change, isn't it?"

The knot in my stomach tightens, but I force a smile, pretending I don't feel the ground crumbling beneath us.

"Hey," I say softly, cupping her cheeks in my hands. "You're my best friend. You'll always be my best friend."

I can still hear her giggle from that first day we met. She had a fuzzy caterpillar in her hand and ran over to show me. I remember the way her freckled nose scrunched up as the caterpillar crawled across her arm. I'd never seen anyone so fascinated by something so small.

The slam of the front door startles us apart. My pulse stutters as heavy boots clomp against the hardwood floor downstairs. I know that sound. I barely have time to react before Dad's voice booms up the staircase.

"James, are you up?"

"Shit," I mutter, pushing off the bed. "Just... stay here."

I slip out of my room and pull the door shut behind me. Dad stands at the top of the stairs, his uniform still on. His tired eyes flick to me, then to my closed door, his jaw tightening.

"James," he says, his voice dangerously even. "Who's in your room?"

Lying isn't an option. Not with him.

"Betty," I say, trying to keep my voice steady. "She just needed to talk."

"You know the rules." His gaze sharpens. "No girls in your room."

"Dad, come on." I grit my teeth. "It's not like that."

"Well, you can thank your sister for making me enforce this rule in the first place." He rubs a hand down his face before glancing at the door again.

"Betty," he calls, his voice a little softer. "Come on out."

The door creaks open, and Betty steps out, her arms wrapped around herself. Her eyes are still puffy and red, but she manages to carve out a weak smile.

"I'm sorry, Mr. Cohen," she says, wiping her eyes. "I know I shouldn't have come so early, but I—" She swallows hard.

Something shifts in my dad's face. The edge softens. Maybe it's the tears on Betty's cheeks or the slight tremble in her voice. Maybe it's because he's known her since we were four. He exhales, shoulders sagging, and then he looks at me.

"Walk her home," he says gruffly. "And next time, James, find somewhere else to talk."

I nod and lead her down the stairs.

"I'm sorry I got you in trouble," she murmurs.

"You didn't." I take her hand. "And besides, you needed me. I'm always going to be here for you. I promise."

I say it for her. But mostly, I say it for me. Because I need to believe that this foreboding distance won't change anything.

Chapter 3
new york city

Betty

It's been six weeks and three days since I was cruelly ripped away from my home. The morning I left Gallipolis is seared into my memory. I packed sixteen years of my life into a suitcase and watched James shrink in the rearview mirror as we drove further and further away from him.

Now I wake up in Greenwich Village. My room is so small, and at times, the walls seem to close in on me, a constant reminder that I'm trapped in this place. The noise here is incessant; horns blaring, people shouting, footsteps echoing off the concrete. Everything feels so fast, too loud. And I'm stuck, trying to find my footing.

I started junior year at St. Cecilia a few weeks ago, and the school is too polished, too perfect. Even the desks are spotless. No carved initials. No doodles. Just more proof this place has no soul. Back in Gallipolis, everything was scuffed and worn. The lockers were dented from years of being slammed shut, and the PA system cut out half the time.

Everyone struts around here in their crisp uniforms, while I feel like an imposter in mine, tugging at the hem of this blazer that doesn't even fit right. No one has tried to talk to me except for Carrigan Montgomery.

I don't know why she chose me, out of the hundreds of girls

at this school, to terrorize. I heard rumors that her mom is an alum, practically St. Cecilia royalty, and Carrigan's been groomed to be this legacy princess, primed to meet every impossible expectation. Maybe, in her own sick way, Carrigan feels threatened by me — a nobody from Ohio.

Walking into school, I see Carrigan waiting for me by my locker. The mood ring on my index finger flares red.

"Hey, Carrot Head," she sneers with her sharp, piercing voice.

For a moment, I consider just walking away, keeping my head down like always. But today, something inside me snaps. Maybe it's the homesickness, the loneliness, or the constant gnawing feeling that I don't belong here. Whatever it is, I've had enough.

"Carrigan," I say, facing her, hands quivering. "What is your problem? *Why* do you hate me?"

Carrigan's large green eyes widen in shock before narrowing into slits. Then she smirks, stepping forward.

"It's pronounced CARE-ih-gin, not CAR-uh-gin." She leans in. "You might wanna remember that if you're planning on sticking around."

Before I can decide what to say next, the bell shrieks through the hallway. I flick my middle finger up, never taking a glance back, and walk straight to class.

As the days blur into weeks, I focus on putting one foot in

front of the other. During lunch, I hide away in the library, drowning myself in books that transport me far away. But sometimes, even the stories can't distract me from reality.

"You've got to at least make an effort," Dad says to me.

"I'm trying."

But what does that even mean anymore? I've done everything they've asked: smiled at the right people, sat at the crowded lunch tables. But what's the point of trying when nothing is working?

"I wish you'd let me call James." My voice falters, and I quickly look away. "I just... I just want to talk to him."

Dad looks up from his newspaper, his brows furrowing. "We've talked about this. Long-distance calls aren't cheap, and I know you two would be on the phone for hours every day."

While I may not be able to hear his voice, I have his handwritten letters. They are the only thing tethering me to home, like a small piece of Gallipolis that I can hold onto. I don't tell him everything — not the bad parts, at least, because the truth feels like too much right now.

October 11, 1997

Dear James,

It's 8 o'clock — usually the time we'd grab a late-night hot chocolate from Marg's. I miss that. I miss you.

St. Cecilia has been an adjustment. The workload is intense, but I'm doing my best to keep up. I've even managed to make a few friends, though none of them can ever replace you.

Last week, my parents took me to the Statue of Liberty. She's smaller than I imagined.

But enough about me — how are you? How's school? Did the football team win the homecoming game?

P.S. I got your mixtape. Rhiannon was a good addition.

With all my love,
Betty

I slip my arms into James's cable-knit cardigan, cradling it close to breathe in the smell of him. Nestled in my bed, staring at the cracks in the ceiling, I wonder if tomorrow will be different. Maybe tomorrow, I'll convince Dad to let me call James.

I close my eyes, drowning out the muffled sounds of the city just beyond my window. The autumn chill is slowly creeping in, but I try to remember the feeling of summer back home.

The damp earth after a thunderstorm. Wildflowers tangled in tall grass. Singing cicadas. Dancing lightning bugs. The humming creek. And James is still there. Waiting for me.

Chapter 4

autumn

James

The fluorescent light flickers above me as I stack boxes of cereal, counting each one like it might somehow add up to something that matters. A plane ticket. A phone call. A visit. A distraction. Anything to drown out the constant ache of missing her.

I want to be angry at her. That she got out. That she's in New York City, where the possibilities are as big as the skyscrapers. Meanwhile, I'm still here bagging groceries at Al's Market, watching the same sun set over the same damn river. I can't be angry at her. It's not her fault.

Still.

I wish we'd started junior year together. And selfishly? I wish her dad hadn't taken that job in New York.

My hands go through the motions — cereal box, shelf, repeat — but my head's still stuck on that late August morning. Standing in the driveway, holding back tears, watching her car shrink into the distance.

"You seem a little distracted today," Al says, jolting me from my thoughts.

Al is a big guy with a booming laugh who's been running this market longer than I've been alive. His peppered gray hair is always slightly disheveled, and his apron is stained with remnants of the day's work — coffee, maybe soup, and a smudge of powdered sugar near the pocket.

"Yeah, I guess I am... a little," I say, my cheeks tinged with embarrassment.

He leans against the counter, arms crossed. "Is it that girlfriend of yours?"

I stop stacking, dropping my head with a heavy nod.

Al softens and steps closer, placing a gentle hand on my shoulder. "Listen, kid. If it's weighing on you this much, you owe it to yourself, and to her, to be honest about how you're feeling."

I let out a heavy sigh. "I just... I keep thinking that if I stay busy, focus on other things, it'll get easier."

Al shakes his head with a chuckle. "You can't just bury something like that and expect it to disappear."

I turn back to the boxes of cereal and start counting again. One, two, three...

Later that night, the phone rings.

My sister has this habit of getting in my business, especially when it comes to my personal life. After Mom died, just two weeks after my bar mitzvah, Julie stepped up, like she had to fill the gap Mom left behind, while Dad kind of shut down, throwing himself into his work. Julie was only sixteen at the time, but everything landed on her shoulders.

"You need to keep your options open," Julie says gently. "I

wasted a whole summer on a guy, and you know what? He forgot about me by fall."

"You don't get it." My voice tightens, like a rubber band ready to snap. "You dated like half of the football team by the time you graduated."

"You think I don't understand?" There's a slight pause, then she continues. "I didn't love any of those guys the way you love Betty. I just don't want you to get hurt."

"You don't have to worry about me so much, Jules," I say, my voice clipped. "You're not Mom."

"I'm your sister." Before I can muster any sort of rebuttal, she adds, "But I'll stop bugging you now."

The line clicks off, leaving me in the silence of my room.

I glance out my window at Betty's empty house across the street. The sight of the dark windows gives me a strange feeling. Back when we were kids, Betty and I had this thing where we'd signal each other using our lights like Morse code. The memory makes me smile, but it quickly fades as I sit back in my chair, thinking back to what Julie said on the phone.

I wish I could talk to Betty face-to-face. The letters are fine, but they only give me fragments of the full picture. At times, I feel like she isn't telling me everything, which makes me wonder — is she feeling the same way?

I grab a pen and begin to write.

November 12, 1997

Dear Betty,

I've written and rewritten this letter at least a dozen times, trying to put into words all this stuff that's been weighing on my mind lately. We've been apart for almost three months, and I've been trying to keep myself busy, you know?

But every time I think I've distracted myself enough, something small happens, and suddenly, it feels like I'm trapped on a sinking ship. I guess what I'm trying to say is, are you feeling the distance too, or am I just overthinking this?

P.S. I drove past Mr. Garver's yesterday. He added another gnome to the collection.

Sincerely,

James

Chapter 5

confetti

Betty

I sit at my desk, staring blankly at the blackboard while Mr. Whitaker drones on about the Pythagorean theorem. The dull throb of a headache starts behind my eyes, barely noticeable at first but slowly growing as the minutes tick by.

I glance back, drawn by the sound of muffled laughter. Carrigan sits a few rows behind me, her eyes locked on mine with that smug grin she always wears. Then suddenly, a paper ball hits the back of my head. Cheeks burning, I keep my eyes glued to my notebook. I won't give her that satisfaction.

When the bell rings, I shove my books into my bag, eager to escape, but just as I'm halfway out of my seat, Mr. Whitaker's voice stops me.

"Betty," he calls, adjusting his horn-rimmed glasses. "Can I talk to you for a moment?"

I slip into the nearest desk at the front, my heart beating a little faster as I wait for him to continue.

"I've noticed your grades have been slipping," Mr. Whitaker starts, his neck bowed over a stack of papers on his desk. Then, he looks up, lowering his voice. "It's normal to struggle a bit when adjusting to a new school, but if you ever want to talk or need help catching up, my door is always open."

I shift uncomfortably, feeling the weight of his gaze boring into me. "Thanks, Mr. Whitacker, but I'm fine," I manage to say, forcing a weak smile.

He watches me closely, clearly unconvinced, then extends his hand, gesturing to the door in quiet dismissal.

I step out of the classroom, hoping to slip through unnoticed. But, of course, Carrigan is waiting for me, leaning against the lockers.

"Hey, Carrot Head!"

I ignore her, clutching my bag tighter, but the moment I try to walk past, her foot darts out. I trip, the world tilting as my books and papers spill from my bag.

"Oops." Carrigan crouches down next to me. "Guess you weren't watching where you were going!"

I scramble to gather my belongings, fighting back the sting of tears. That's when I see one of James's letters lying among the clutter. Before I can grab it, Carrigan's fingers snatch it up.

"What's this?" She stands, holding the wrinkled paper.

"Give it back," I snap, my voice trembling as I reach for it.

Carrigan straightens with a wicked smirk, then bolts down the hallway. I chase after her, weaving through the throng of students who barely move aside.

The bathroom door swings shut behind me as I burst in, my breath coming in short, ragged gasps. She's standing by the sinks, a triumphant grin on her face, waving the letter around like a trophy.

"You want this?"

"Carrigan, plea—"

The words die in my throat as she tears the paper in half. Then again. And again, until the pieces flutter to the floor like confetti. Carrigan slithers out of the bathroom without another word.

I sink to the floor, my knees hitting the tiles with a dull thud. My hands tremble as I pick up the fragments piece by piece. A flicker of color catches my eye: my mood ring, dull and dark. I don't need to look twice to know it's black, stark against my pale skin.

I stumble out of the bathroom. My tear-filled eyes scan the empty hallway before landing on the fluorescent EXIT sign above the main doors. I just need to go home, where I can bury myself under blankets, where I don't have to think, where I don't have to hear the icy laughter of Carrigan.

By the time I reach the apartment, my headache is pounding. Dropping my bag by the front door, I retreat to my room. I pull out a sheet of paper and begin to write, the words spilling out in a sloppy rush.

November 19, 1997

Dear James,

I need to tell you the truth.

I haven't made any friends. Not one. I try to pretend I'm okay, but the truth is, I'm not. I read your letters so many times, I've memorized every word. I wish I could go back to that summer day we carved our names into the tree and stay there forever.

Yours always,
Betty

Taking a deep breath, I drop the letter into the mail slot. I turn, watching the wind scatter the leaves across the pavement like the pieces of the letter I couldn't save.

Chapter 6
the 3rd of december
James

Julie swings the door open, a pile of mail in her arms. Stepping inside, she kicks off her boots, leaving tiny puddles of melted snow by the mat, and tosses her keys onto the table with a clatter.

"Anything for me?" I ask, glancing up from my geometry textbook.

She flips through the stack of holiday greeting cards and utility bills, then shakes her head.

It's been nearly a month since I last heard from Betty. With each passing day, I feel a little more hopeless. Maybe... maybe Betty has moved on. At least, that's what Julie's been telling me ever since she got home for winter break.

"Girls are very open when it comes to their feelings," she says. "I hate to say it, but maybe she's already made up her mind."

"Maybe she's just busy," I reply, trying to sound more confident than I feel.

"Too busy to reply to your letter?" She rolls her eyes, nudging me with a playful grin. "Come on, James — it's the holidays. I'm tired of seeing you mope around. Just go out and let yourself have fun."

I sigh, dropping my head.

Julie watches me for a moment, then changes the subject. "What are you doing Friday night?" She plops down next to me. "Wanna have an early birthday celebration? Maybe we can hit up Blockbuster and have a horror movie marathon."

"Why not a Christmas movie?"

She snorts. "Too cliché."

"Sounds fun, but I can't," I say, eyes glued to the math equations that make no sense. "I'm volunteering at something for school."

She stands, ruffling my hair with a smile. "Well, alright. I'll let you finish studying. Just try not to fry your brain in the process."

Finals week comes and goes. I do okay — average grades, like I expect. But geometry, as always, remains my downfall. At least it's finally winter break.

Every year, the high school organizes volunteer events that students are required to participate in. Betty and I always signed up for the toy drive. I remember how we'd always end up working together in the same corner of the gym, hunched over a table.

Betty was always so meticulous, folding the wrapping paper just right, adding little ribbons and bows. I'd tease her about making every gift look like it belonged in a Sears catalog, but she'd just smile, saying, "It's the little things that make a difference."

This year, I signed up to volunteer at the local soup kitchen, mostly because some friends had signed up, and I didn't want to be the odd one out.

Walking through the doors, I duck my head under the paper snowflakes hanging from the ceiling. Miles is already here, arranging tables.

Miles Cooper isn't the kind of guy I'd normally call a friend. Yet, after two years of being on the student council together, I've come to realize there's more to him than his loud, boisterous exterior. He's surprisingly smart. Insightful, even. The kind of guy who can make a whole classroom burst into laughter but still remembers your birthday.

As I begin unfolding chairs next to him, I notice a girl wiping down tables nearby, swaying to whatever song is playing through her headphones. Her blonde ponytail swings with every move... and the way she moves. It's effortless, natural.

I nudge Miles. "Who is that?"

"Cassie Parker," he replies, glancing over. "She's new this year. A sophomore."

"What do you know about her?" I ask, my voice slightly catching.

"Not much. Just that her folks moved here over the summer, and she's a ballerina."

"A ballerina?"

"Yeah, she's pretty cute, huh?" Miles says, nudging me as we both watch her for a moment. "Come on."

Before I can protest, his hand lands on my shoulder, and he steers me toward her. She doesn't notice us right away; she's still caught in whatever song she's listening to, wiping the table in a steady rhythm.

Miles knocks on the table three times. She jolts a little, tugging her headphones off. Her eyes flick up.

"This is my buddy, James," Miles says with a grin. "Figured you two should meet."

Cassie smiles, brushing a strand of hair behind her ear.

We work side by side, ladling bowls of butternut squash soup together. By the time 8:00 PM rolls around, I've spent the last three hours working up the courage to say something to her. But at the same time, I've spent the last three hours wondering what Betty is doing. Is she thinking about me?

As Cassie heads for the door, I sling my bag over my shoulder and jog to catch up.

"Hey, Cassie!"

She looks back over her shoulder. "James, right?"

"Yeah, I was wondering—" I don't even know *what* I'm doing. "Do you want to grab something to eat?"

Cassie pauses, and with a smile, she nods.

I help Cassie into the passenger seat of my truck, and for a moment, I'm embarrassed by the amount of rust eating away at the door. As I settle into the driver's seat, I steal a glance at her, my mind scrambling for something—anything to say.

I steer us toward Marg's Diner, and as I pull into a spot, the truck settles into a quiet hum. Inside, we slide into a booth in the back corner. I look at the clock, 8:25 P.M., and realize I'd normally be here... drinking hot chocolate... with Betty.

Dolly shuffles over, a cigarette dangling from her lips. "Hot chocolate for you, James?" She turns to Cassie. "And what about you, blondie?"

"I'll take a slice of cherry pie," Cassie replies with a smile.

Dolly scribbles down the order and ambles back into the kitchen, her footsteps slow and heavy.

"So," I begin, leaning forward, "what brought you to Gallipolis?"

She hesitates, glancing at the floor before speaking. "Well, my mom grew up here," she says. "We moved into her childhood home on Oakwood Avenue."

I suddenly recall that summer day, driving down Oakwood Avenue with Betty and spotting a moving truck parked on the street.

"No way," I exclaim, eyes wide with realization. "You... *you're* the one who moved into the old Reynold's house?"

Cassie raises an eyebrow. "I guess so?"

I sink back in the booth. "You know, people say that house is haunted?"

She snorts. "Haunted? Really?"

"Hey, who doesn't love a good ghost story? Even the legend of Mothman still creeps into conversations around here." I lean in. "Okay, humor me. Why Gallipolis of all places?"

She hesitates, biting her lip. "I think my parents just wanted a change. A quieter life, perhaps."

"Well, it *is* quiet around here, that's for sure."

"But I like it."

I can't help but laugh, shaking my head. "I can't wait to get out of here."

"Really? Why?"

"Why?" I repeat, letting out a quiet snort. Then I sink back in my seat. "There used to be more here for me, I guess."

Dolly returns, setting down the mug of hot chocolate and plate of cherry pie between us with a heavy thud, the silverware rattling slightly.

"I haven't had much time to explore the town," Cassie says, gliding her fork through the cherry syrup pooling on her plate.

"Well, there's not much to see," I begin, "but I could show you around sometime. Maybe we can catch that new *Scream* movie... if you're up for it?"

I feel a faint tremor under the table, a vibration running through the floor. Glancing down, I notice Cassie's leg bouncing nervously.

She bites her lip, her eyes flitting away as if trying to find the right words. "Can I think about it?"

I pick up my mug, the last sip of hot chocolate now lukewarm. I want to say something to keep this moment from slipping away. My mind races, and for a second, I think about just letting her walk out of here without trying. But then, I hear Julie in my head again — annoying how she's always right.

My gaze drops to the napkin in front of me, my chest tightening as I grab it. With a trembling hand, I scribble down my phone number. "Give me a call whenever you're ready," I say, sliding the napkin across the table.

Cassie takes the napkin, her fingers briefly brushing mine. Her lips curve into a small, hesitant smile. "I should probably head home," she says, glancing out the window. "But thank you, James... for tonight."

She rises from the booth and turns toward the door, the napkin tucked safely in her pocket. I stay rooted to my seat, watching her leave. As the door jingles shut behind her, I realize I'm not quite sure what tonight meant, but I know it meant something.

Chapter 7
mcgregor's nook
Betty

Every day, my eyes drift toward the post box, and every day, my stomach tightens when I find it empty yet again. At first, I held onto hope, half-expecting to see an envelope tucked inside with my name on it.

But after weeks of disappointment, I've learned it's best not to expect anything at all. For a while, it felt like I was walking through a drought, looking up at the sky, and praying for rain that would never come.

I have pages filled with words I'll probably never send him. They sit folded in the back of my journal, ink smudged from where my sweaty hands paused too long, scribbling over sentences I wasn't sure I meant.

I don't know if I should send them. Maybe James has moved on, and I'm the only one still holding on. Maybe his feelings for me have changed, and I just haven't caught up yet.

I've taken to wandering around Greenwich Village, hoping that with each step I take, I can ease the ache in my heart, which stubbornly clings to me. My walks always start at The Beanery, where the cappuccinos are perfect, though their hot chocolate pales next to Marg's.

I loop around the Washington Square Fountain, counting my tracks in the snow. The cold seeps through my mittens, leaving my fingers numb. On my third lap around the fountain, it hits me—

Tomorrow is James's seventeenth birthday.

I picture him sitting at the kitchen table, blowing out candles while his dad grumbles about the price of a store-bought cake and Julie loudly sings "Happy Birthday" off-key on purpose. I used to be there for all of it.

His birthday always landed in the middle of Hanukkah, and even though I'm Catholic, Mrs. Cohen always welcomed me into the celebration with open arms. We'd light the menorah, then eat birthday cake while the smell of homemade latkes lingered in the air.

After his mom passed, Hanukkah felt different. I could see it in James, the way he stared at the menorah's flames, distant and withdrawn. What had once been a season of stories and tradition felt quieter, dimmer, like the light she brought to their home had faded with her.

Eventually, I find myself at the window of McGregor's Nook, a bookshop on Waverly Street. The glow of yellow light spills onto the snowy sidewalk, pulling me in before I even realize I've opened the door.

I run my fingers along the spines of the dull-colored books and reach for a poetry collection.

My thumb skims over a line: *Hope is the thing with feathers.*

My chest tightens, and I snap the book shut.

"That one's a classic," a voice calls out from behind the counter.

I glance up. A man steps into view, his hands tucked into his pockets. His hair is white like a ghost, and his wrinkles deepen as he smiles.

He gestures to the book in my hands. "You've got good taste." He studies me for a moment, cocking his head with curiosity, and continues, "Do you have a favorite?"

I don't hesitate. "The Great Gatsby," I say, stepping toward him. "The idea of chasing a dream... even when it feels impossible. Fitzgerald had a way of capturing the hope in people's hearts."

Suddenly, an orange cat tiptoes around the corner, rubbing against my leg. I smile, reaching down to stroke the cat.

"This is Fitzgerald," the man says gently. "Named after the very author you mentioned." He holds out his hand. "And I'm Edwin McGregor."

"It's a pleasure to meet you," I say, shaking it. "I'm Betty."

He leans in slightly, grinning. "So Betty, are you from the city?"

"No, I'm from Gallipolis."

"Gallipolis," he echoes, sounding out each syllable. "You'll have to point that out on a map for me."

"Most people do. Blink, and you'd miss it."

Mr. McGregor's eyes crinkle with amusement. "Do you miss it?" he asks, resting his elbows on the counter.

"Sometimes I try to pretend the noise outside is cicadas," I say softly. "But it never sounds quite right."

The silence that follows isn't awkward — just easy. Like he understands. He hums in thought, glancing down at the stack of books beside him. His fingers skim along the spines before settling on a slim, hardbound book.

"Have you ever read Sylvia Plath?"

"No, I haven't," I say, intrigued.

"Sylvia Plath was quite the enigma," he says, handing me *The Bell Jar*. "A writer ahead of her time."

I fumble around in my bag for my wallet, but then he stops me, holding up his hand with a smile.

"Merry Christmas, Betty," he says warmly.

"Merry Christmas, Mr. McGregor."

As I leave the bookshop, clutching my new treasure, I wrap my red scarf around my neck. For the first time in months, I feel a tiny flicker of hope, like the soft glow of candles in a menorah; small, but persistent against the darkness.

Chapter 8
new year's eve
James

The day after Christmas, Cassie called. Her voice surprised me. Lighter, softer than I remembered. For a moment, I almost didn't recognize it. We talked for hours, and at some point, an invitation to a New Year's Eve party slipped out. To my surprise, Cassie agreed to come with me.

I pull up to her house, my pulse quickening as I spot her on the sagging porch. She looks hesitant, hands stuffed in her coat pockets, head bowed against the cold. I lean on the horn three times.

Cassie's head snaps up, and she hurries toward my truck. "Why did you do that?" she asks, her eyes narrowing.

I grip the wheel, trying to laugh it off. "It's just an old habit."

"Please don't honk your horn at me," she says, climbing into the seat. "It felt like you were whistling at me. Like I was a dog."

"No, that's not —" I begin, my voice faltering. "Look, I'm sorry. I won't do it again."

As we drive along, the silence in the truck is deafening, broken only by the roar of the exhaust. I steal a glance at her, wondering what she's thinking. Now and then, I inch my hand closer to hers, but then I hesitate and pull away.

When we arrive at the party, I guide Cassie through the crowd, my grip on her hand tightening as we walk toward the drink table. Lights are strung up along the windows, and the odor of beer mingles with cheap cologne.

I grab a beer and glance at Cassie filling a cup with Coke. "Don't you drink?"

Cassie's expression stiffens. "No," she responds, her voice flat. "And besides the fact that I'm sixteen, I've seen what too much wine does to my mom."

I try to lighten the mood, leaning against the table with a chuckle. "Stick around this town a few more years, and it'll give you a good excuse to drink."

I expect her to laugh, but she doesn't. Instead, her gaze hardens. She doesn't say anything, just sips her Coke in silence. I open my mouth to apologize, realizing too late how stupid that sounded, but no words come.

A group of lacrosse players hurls past us. One of them, clearly not paying attention, bumps into Cassie, spilling his beer on her.

"Hey man, are you serious?!" My hand grabs his shoulder.

Miles turns and staggers back a few steps. "Shit, didn't see you there." He blinks, looking between the two of us, then grins. "Hey, look at you two. Guess my matchmaking worked out, huh?" With a chuckle, he raises his bottle in salute and stumbles off.

I turn back to Cassie. "Sorry about him." I take her hand gently. "Come on. Let's get you cleaned up."

I shut the bathroom door behind us, muffling the noise of the party. Grabbing some towels from under the cabinet, I begin dabbing at the stains on her dress.

I feel stupid for inviting her to this party. I don't even know why she agreed to come with me. But despite everything, Cassie's standing still, letting me clean her up, and that's something, I guess.

"Sorry," I murmur, dabbing at the stain. "I didn't mean for the night to go like this."

She glances down at herself. The stain is still there, but she shrugs and steps toward the door. "Come on, it's almost midnight."

She looks up at me, her smile finally surfacing for the first time all night. We make our way back to the party, and when we step into the living room, the countdown is already starting.

Five... four...three...two...one.

Cassie steps on her tiptoes and kisses me. For a moment, all I can taste is the watermelon chapstick lingering on her lips. But then, like a jolt, Betty's face flashes in my mind, vivid — and suddenly, all I can think about is how everything about tonight feels wrong. My chest tightens as I feel something shift in the air around us. I take a step back, my eyes dropping to the floor.

Cassie watches me, then her hand finds mine, squeezing it gently as she pulls me toward the door. Outside, the air is cold, biting against my skin. She shivers beside me, wrapping her arms around herself. Without thinking, I take off my jacket and drape it over her shoulders.

"James, is everything alright?"

I look at her, seeing the doubt form behind her eyes.

"When I kissed you," she continues, "it felt like... I don't know. Like you weren't really there."

Say something, you idiot. Do something. Instead, I glance away, my gaze landing on the frozen river in the distance.

The drive back is quiet. I briefly glance at her, searching for something, some sign that she's okay, but all I see is her retreating into herself, staring out of the window.

I pull up to her house, where Cassie promptly slides out of the truck. As she glances back with a slight smile, it hits me—

I can't let her leave like this.

I jump out of the truck and sprint after her, the words spilling out before I can even gather my thoughts. "I don't... I don't know what I'm doing. And I don't know what *this* is yet, but I know I don't want to screw it up."

For a moment, she just stares at me. Then, she turns, glancing back one last time before stepping onto the porch, the front door closing behind her.

Chapter 9
to the lighthouse
Betty

The Bell Jar hasn't left me. Its words linger, clinging to every corner of my mind. Since finishing it, I've been hungry for more—more stories, more words, more voices that seem to understand the quiet parts of me.

Mr. McGregor keeps slipping me books, and lately, I've started sharing pieces of my poetry with him. Just the small ones. And only when I'm feeling brave.

Today is one of those days. My fingers drum nervously on his desk, trying to mask the butterflies while Mr. McGregor reads my poem. His eyes finally lift to meet mine, and he smiles, a warm, encouraging smile.

"Brilliant," Mr. McGregor says, handing me back the journal. "You've got a talent."

Before I can respond, the door chimes behind me. I glance up and see a younger guy, tall, with black curls, shaking off the rain from his umbrella. I turn my attention back to Mr. McGregor, though something about the mysterious bookstore guy catches my attention.

"Have you ever thought about pursuing this as a career?"

I shake my head. "I don't even know where I'd start."

He places his hand in his pocket and pulls out a small, crimson lapel pin.

"Start here," Mr. McGregor says, sliding it across the desk. "Cornell University: Class of 1945," he states proudly. "I studied English Literature."

The idea of college seems so far out of reach, like something meant for people smarter, more driven than me. I try to picture myself there, walking across the ivy-covered campus, surrounded by students who seem so much more sure about their futures than I'll ever be. It feels impossible, like imagining myself on the moon.

Yet, later that night at the dinner table, I ask, "What do you think about Cornell University?"

"It's expensive," Dad quickly states.

"George," Mom admonishes, before turning her focus to me. "Are you thinking about applying there?"

I fidget with the food on my plate, dragging my fork through the mashed potatoes. "I don't know. Maybe."

Mom exchanges a glance with Dad before turning back to me. "Betty, we got a call from your school today."

Oh no. She never calls me Betty. Always Goose. Or sometimes Goosie, if she's feeling sweet. Whatever she's going to say next isn't good.

"About your grades."

My throat tightens. I stare at my plate, the meatloaf muddling in my vision.

"Your education is important, especially if you're thinking

about applying to a school like Cornell University," Mom says, her voice firmer now. "Betty, what's going on?"

"I have no friends," I whisper, as if saying it out loud might make it worse.

Dad sighs, pushing his chair back slightly. "It takes time. Just try again."

"Try again?" I snap. "*That's* your advice? How exactly do you expect me to make friends when I'm stuck in classes with girls like Carrigan Montgomery, who make my life a living hell every single day? You want me to buddy up with *her*?" I loudly sigh, throwing my head back in frustration.

"Betty, that's not—" Dad starts, but I cut him off.

"You don't get it!" My hands clench into fists. "You have no idea how much I hate it here!"

There's a stunned silence. Dad shifts in his seat, his firm expression faltering.

"Betty," he starts, his voice breaking through the quiet, "you have to understand that —"

"No!" I snap, pushing back my chair with a sharp scrape. "You act like I'm supposed to be fine about everything. But I didn't ask for any of this!" My voice wavers, but I keep going, the words tumbling out. "I didn't ask to leave Gallipolis, or my school... or James."

My voice cracks on the last word.

Tears sting at the corners of my eyes, but I push forward.

"You uprooted my entire life and didn't bother to ask if I was okay. Do you even care about me?"

Dad's eyes fix on me, unwavering. "Of course we care," he starts, his voice quieter than before. "But we didn't make this decision lightly and—"

I bolt from the table, my footsteps echoing down the hallway. I throw open the door to my bedroom and slam it shut behind me, the sound reverberating through the apartment.

Why won't they listen to me? Why hasn't James written to me? Why did I have to leave Gallipolis? Why this city, this school, this life I never asked for?

The questions swirl in my head, colliding like a tornado I can't outrun. I collapse face-first onto my bed, eyes squeezed shut as I scream into my pillow.

I think about the novel *To The Lighthouse* and how the Ramsays are a lot like my own parents. Mom is a lot like Mrs. Ramsay. She has this way of making everything feel warm and safe. I felt it in the way she patched me up with gentle hands whenever I scraped my knee on the concrete. I felt it in the way I'd lay my head in her lap while she sang to me, running her fingers through my hair.

And much like Mr. Ramsay, Dad is often stone-cold. He's the most intelligent man I've ever met, though I know he doesn't understand me. I don't blame him. It can be hard to interpret the inner workings of a sixteen-year-old girl's mind.

Suddenly, there's a knock — the door creaks open, and Dad peeks in. "Hey, squirt. Mind if I come in?"

I sit up, meeting his gaze with a nod.

Dad walks over to my bed, perching on the edge, his weight causing the mattress to dip slightly. His eyes scan the room, taking in the mess of scattered books and clothes that seem to mirror the turmoil in my mind.

"Betty," he begins, his eyes softening, "I know that nothing about this move has been easy on you. I know you're angry. And I know how much you miss home."

I stare at him, unsure of how to respond. We've never had a heart-to-heart like this. It's just not something he's good at. And yet, I feel something shift in his presence. Maybe he doesn't understand it all, but he's trying. And that means something.

"Why didn't you tell us how bad it was at school?"

"I don't know," I mutter quietly.

Dad exhales sharply. "Look, I know how tough things can be at your age. I'll make a call to the school on Monday and talk to the headmaster about this Carrie girl."

"Carrigan."

"Right, Carrigan," Dad repeats, nodding. "How about we make a deal?" His gaze meets mine. "Get your grades back up, then you can call James."

I hesitate, a small smile tugging at my lips. "Deal."

"That's my girl," he whispers, straightening up and heading for the door.

"Dad?" I call just as he's about to leave.

He pauses, glancing back.

"I love you."

"I love you, too, squirt."

I pull my cardigan tighter around me. Not to hide, but to hold on.

Chapter 10
the old reynold's house
James

When school started back up after the holiday break, things with Cassie began... slowly. I figured I'd blown it at that New Year's Eve party. But on the first day back from break, there she was, waiting at my locker like nothing had changed.

After that, I started walking her to class, sitting next to her at lunch, and occasionally meeting at her locker after school — small things like that. But then one day in February, she asked if I wanted to study at her house later that night.

I've noticed how different Cassie is from Betty. Betty always filled the silence, whether with words, laughter, or lyrics from a song playing on the radio. And even when she wasn't saying anything, I could read her like a book in the way she scrunched her nose when she was annoyed or how she tapped her fingers against her leg when she was nervous. With Betty, there were never any guessing games.

Cassie's different. She's quieter, harder to read. But maybe that's why I'm so drawn to her. She keeps herself guarded, like she's afraid of what might happen if she lets someone get too close. With Betty, I always knew where I stood. With Cassie, I feel like I'm walking through fog, trying to find my footing.

And yet, I can't seem to look away.

Stepping into her bedroom, balancing a stack of books in

one hand and a bag of chips in the other, I see Cassie, surrounded by piles of notebooks and papers. She looks up from her bed, her face lighting up with a smile.

"I brought reinforcements." I drop the bag of chips onto the bed. "So, where do you want to start? Math or Science? Neither's exactly my strong suit."

She laughs, reaching into the bag of chips. "Let's tackle math first. Maybe when we're done, we can treat ourselves to a snack break."

I settle onto the bed across from Cassie, opening my textbook, though my gaze keeps drifting around the room, eyes wide with wonder. Cassie's room is... unexpected.

Warm. Yet cold.

Lived-in. Yet abandoned.

There's a stack of books on the windowsill. A pair of pointe shoes dangle from a nail above the closet door, the ribbons faded, the toes worn. The wallpaper is peeling in one corner, curling away from the wall like it's trying to leave.

It's weird being here — in *this* house, of all houses. I remember riding past it on my bike when I was a kid, thinking it looked like something out of a horror movie. Now I'm sitting in one of its upstairs bedrooms, where the floor creaks and the windows rattle as if someone is trying to break in.

She catches me looking around. "What is it?"

"I can't believe I'm here... in this house." I shake my head.

Cassie chuckles. "It's just a house, James."

It's not *just* a house.

It's the legendary Reynold's house on Oakwood Avenue. Betty would lose her mind if she knew. She used to make up stories about this place. Said the attic was full of haunted ancient Egyptian artifacts. I always laughed, but part of me believed her. One time, she dared me to ding-dong ditch it, but I was too chicken to even step onto the porch.

Leaning in, I raise an eyebrow, my interest piqued. "Any ghost stories so far?"

Cassie bites her lip, feigning deep thought. "No, but I promise I'll let you know if I start hearing any strange noises." She grins, then adds, "Now, come on. I really like you, and I don't want you to fail geometry."

I reach into my pocket, hands shaking, as I hand her a cassette tape. "I made you this mixtape... to thank you for tutoring me."

"You made this for me?"

I nod. "Late nights, lots of rewinding. Wore out half of my dad's tapes putting it together."

Turning it over in her hand, her eyes scan through my messy handwriting. "The Zombies. Patti Smith. The Byrds." Her voice softens. "You have really good taste."

I shrug. "Thought you'd like it."

"I do." She looks at me, smiling. "I love it."

I glance up when I hear muffled footsteps coming down the hallway. Cassie perks up, scrambling to her feet.

"Mom... Dad, I want you to meet James!"

Her mom glances our way, offering a polite smile. Her dad doesn't even make eye contact, brushing past us as if we're part of the furniture. Cassie's smile disappears completely as she watches them disappear down the hall. Slowly, she turns back to me, the brightness in her eyes gone.

For a few moments, neither of us says anything. Cassie stares at the page in front of her, her fingers lightly tapping the edge of her pencil. Part of me wants to just dive into these math problems and let the moment pass, but there's something about Cassie, sitting there, shoulders slumped, that makes it impossible.

"Cassie," I start, clearing my throat. "Are you okay?"

Her eyes drift up from her notebook. "Yeah, I'm fine." And then, her gaze drops again. She lets out a breath, her voice quieter now. "Sorry about them. After we moved here, they just... kinda shut down."

I pause, fidgeting with the corner of my textbook. "You know, I get it. My dad shut down, too. After my mom passed."

Cassie doesn't say anything, but she doesn't look away either.

"I was twelve years old when she got sick." I pause, swallowing hard. "At first, I didn't think it was that serious. I was in denial, I guess. But as the months went by, it became clear that she wasn't getting better."

I remember how yellow the light in the kitchen looked, too bright for the moment, as Dad told me that Mom wasn't coming home. I remember how quiet his voice was, as if he was afraid to say it out loud.

I remember the way Julie's hands trembled when she handed my lunch to me, the paper bag crinkling under her grip as she tried to act like everything was normal. But I saw it. I saw it in the way her eyes avoided mine, too scared to look at me directly.

And then there was Betty. She tried to be there for me, but I kept pushing her away. I thought I needed to face my grief alone. She didn't understand why, and honestly, neither did I. But after a while, I realized shutting her out wasn't just lonely — it wasn't fair.

"After she passed," I begin quietly, "my dad... changed. It felt like I lost both of my parents that day."

I remember thinking that if I could scream loud enough, maybe he'd wake up from that trance. But every time I tried to talk to him, his response was always the same—

"Not right now."

She reaches her hand to mine, grasping it tightly. "James, I'm so sorry."

"You said they shut down after the move," I say, clearing

my throat. "Do you know why? I mean, was there... a moment? Like something that flipped the switch?"

Her expression flickers, like a window slamming shut. "We should get back to these math problems." She flips to a new page, eyes locked on the paper.

"Cassie," I say, leaning in. "You can talk to me."

She shakes her head. "Maybe... maybe you should just go."

I want to tell her no, but I see it in her eyes. The desperation. And so, I gather my things. My fingers fumble with the strap of my bag, but I don't leave immediately. I linger at the door, my hand on the knob, waiting for her to tell me to stay.

But she doesn't.

So I open the door, stepping into the hallway, then quietly, I close the door behind me.

Chapter 11
the poetry reading
Betty

With a bit of tutoring and extra credit, I managed to bring my geometry grade up to a B. And whatever Dad said to the headmaster about Carrigan must have done the trick; she's kept her distance for weeks. For the first time, school feels bearable.

"Nice job," Dad says, reading through my report card.

"So, I can call James?"

Dad looks at me, a grin tugging on his lips. "You earned it."

With a squeal of excitement, I rush over to the phone and begin dialing the only number I know by heart. I wait with bated breath as the line rings.

"Pick up," I whisper.

The line clicks to silence, then the voicemail tone. I hang up before it beeps. For a moment, I just stare at the phone.

Maybe he was busy. Maybe he was out. I don't want to overthink it. I *shouldn't* overthink it. And yet—

I beeline it to McGregor's Nook, my backpack weighed down with books. Fitzgerald curls around my legs as I sit in the overstuffed chair in the corner. I chew the end of my pen, scribbling words in my journal that never quite feel right.

The guy with the curly black hair is here again, a pencil tucked behind his ear like he's ready to jot down notes at any moment. It makes me wonder what kind of words speak to him. He always shows up around the same time, always gravitating toward the same shelves, while I stay tucked in my corner, pretending not to notice. But I do. Every. Single. Time.

I watch him out of the corner of my eye. The soft amber glow of the lamplight catches the warmth of his brown skin like honey in a jar. His fingers glide over the spines of the books, like he's searching for something specific. Our eyes meet briefly, then dart away.

Mr. McGregor walks over to me, a flyer in his hand. "Betty, there's a poetry reading coming up. You should think about entering."

I glance at the paper. The event is set for next month at a library in Lower Manhattan.

Suddenly, I hear a voice behind me. "You write poetry?"

I turn to see him, the boy with curly black hair, standing a few feet away, one eyebrow raised.

"Yeah, sort of," I say, feeling my cheeks flush.

"Sort of?" Mr. McGregor laughs. "Betty, you're too modest." He turns to the boy. "You write too?"

Nodding, he takes a step closer. "I dabble a bit."

"Then you should *both* think about signing up," Mr. McGregor says, shuffling back to his desk.

The boy turns back to me. "I've noticed you come here a lot — don't you?"

"It's quiet here." I smile. "And in a weird way, it reminds me of home — even if everything else doesn't."

"Let me guess," he says, leaning in. "Small-town girl moves to the big city. Kentucky?"

"Ohio." I grin, tucking a piece of hair behind my ear.

"Ohio? Never been."

"It's not everyone's cup of tea," I say, smiling softly. "But for me, it's home. It'll always be home." I shift in the overstuffed chair. "This might sound silly, but poetry has helped me find my way."

He leans in closer. "It's not silly at all. Words have a way of pulling you in, taking you somewhere else." He tilts his head, studying me with a thoughtful smile. "Which is why you should sign up for that poetry reading."

I hesitate, still not entirely sure if I'm ready to share my words with the world, let alone with him. I turn my gaze to the pages of my book. "It's not really my type of thing."

He chuckles softly. "Words deserve to be heard. And you seem like someone who has a lot to say."

I glance at the flyer again. For a moment, I imagine it: the microphone, the stage, the room full of strangers. The idea terrifies me, but something in his steady gaze makes it feel possible.

"Okay," I finally say, nodding. "I'll do it."

He smiles, extending his hand toward me. "Simon."

"Betty."

Over the next few weeks, Simon and I meet regularly at McGregor's Nook. It's always casual, conversations about our favorite poets and how certain lines feel like they were written just for us. Simon's thoughtful in a way that surprises me, and it feels good to talk to someone who loves words as much as I do.

When the evening of the poetry reading arrives, I sit near the back, clasping my sweaty hands together to stop them from shaking. Simon is across the room, talking with a group of people, but now and then, he glances over and smiles.

When it's Simon's turn to read, the room goes quiet. His voice is calm and steady, and there's something almost hypnotic about the way he speaks. When he finishes, he gives me a quick smile and steps away from the microphone.

My heart pounds out of my chest, each step to the microphone feeling heavier than the last. The room tilts slightly as I face the crowd, all expectant, all waiting. My fingers clutch the paper so tightly I'm afraid it'll tear.

Why did I agree to this?

I consider running, slipping out the side door, disappearing into the night. But then I spot Simon across the room. His eyes meet mine, steady and warm. Then, he gives me a gentle, reassuring nod.

I take a shaky breath, forcing my gaze to focus on the

crowd in front of me. "Hi, my name is Betty," I begin, my voice slightly faltering. "And this is my poem, *Summer*."

The creek hums,
cool against our skin,
lapping at our ankles,
pulling us deeper, deeper
where time doesn't chase us.
I watch the ripples stretch,
soft rings folding into each other,
disappearing before they reach the shore.
And I wonder if we'll disappear too,
if time will pull us apart
like the current tugging at the reeds?
But then he laughs,
that beautiful laugh,
our bare feet in the shallows,
cicadas singing in the trees,
and tadpoles in my jar.

For a moment, the room is silent. My chest tightens with panic. But then, the applause comes, soft at first, then growing louder, and I let out the breath I didn't realize I was holding.

I step down from the mic, my knees still wobbling, and find a quiet corner beside the snack table. I reach for a napkin, wiping my palms, and glance down. The ring on my finger shifts to purple, like the lilacs that bloom in Grandma's garden.

Simon walks over, a grin on his face. "You were brilliant."

"Thanks," I reply, feeling a flutter in my chest. "You were, too."

He reaches for a cookie but stops, giving me a thoughtful look. "Important question: chocolate chip or snickerdoodle?"

I laugh, a little surprised. "Chocolate chip. Classic."

"Good choice," he says, grabbing a cookie and taking a bite. "So, apart from poetry and cookie insights, are there any other hidden talents I should know about?"

I hesitate, playfully pondering. "I *can* make a pretty mean grilled cheese sandwich."

"Solid skill."

"What about you?" I say, nudging him. "Any hidden talents besides being the mysterious bookstore guy?"

"Mysterious bookstore guy?" He raises an eyebrow, chuckling. "Was that your first impression of me?"

I shrug, a smirk playing on my lips.

He meets my gaze, his expression softening. "Well, how about we grab a coffee sometime, and I'll prove there's more to me than 'mysterious bookstore guy'?"

My breath hitches. I like Simon; he's kind, thoughtful, and being with him feels good, but somehow, it also feels wrong.

"I'd like that, but —" My gaze drops to the floor.

"But?" Simon shifts slightly, studying my face. For a

second, a flicker of something crosses his expression, but he quickly hides it behind an understanding smile. "I-I'm sorry if I got the wrong impression."

"No, no, I just—" I tug at the sleeve of my cardigan.

"Your poem... was it about someone? Someone back home?"

I nod slowly, my gaze lowering to my mood ring. It morphs to a blend of red and orange, like it can't quite decide how I feel either.

He pushes his hands into his pockets, glancing toward the door. "I should get going. But if you ever want to talk or share more poems... you know where to find me."

As Simon walks away, my heart sinks. It's not the idea of moving on that scares me. It's the thought of leaving James behind.

Chapter 12
the treehouse

Cassie

It's been two weeks since I last spoke to James, and in the quiet of my loneliness, a painful truth has settled in: I shouldn't have pushed him away. It wasn't fair to him. He doesn't know the truth about our move to Gallipolis. But I can't tell him.

One thing I *can* do is try to talk to my parents. It's been almost a year since everything happened. Maybe they can come to forgive me, and we can move past everything. To go back to the way things used to be.

With bated breath and trembling hands, I step into the kitchen, the faint smell of cigarettes trapped in the wallpaper. My parents sit at the table, their heads bowed over the newspaper spread out between them.

"Can we talk?" I ask, my voice wavering slightly.

They both look up, but Mom's gaze drops back down to her crossword puzzle almost immediately. The silence stretches on, suffocating me.

"Please," I mutter, my hands quivering at my sides. "We have to talk about this eventually."

Dad sighs, setting down his coffee. "Not right now."

"When?" I say, my voice rising. "When are we going to talk about this?"

Dad's eyes narrow. "Don't raise your voice at us."

"Don't raise my voice?" I scoff, crossing my arms. "What else am I supposed to do to get your attention? You won't even look at me! "

Mom's eyes meet mine with a coldness I've grown all too familiar with. "Do I need to remind you why we're even here?"

My stomach twists. I already know what she's going to say, but hearing it still feels like a slap across the face.

She puffs her cigarette, blowing a plume of smoke. "You embarrassed us, Cassandra. That whole debacle ruined us."

"I was *fifteen*." My voice cracks. "I know I made a mistake. And I wish I could tell her how sorry I am."

"Enough, Cassandra!" Dad slams his hand on the table, rattling the plates and silverware. "Go to your room."

I close my bedroom door behind me, even though I want to slam it with all my might. My hands tremble as I lock it, struggling to calm the tremor in my breath.

I glance toward the window, the pale glow of the streetlamp spilling into my room. I grab my jacket and inch the window open just enough to slip through. My feet hit the grass below, and I take off.

With each step, I feel the weight that's been bearing on my shoulders lifting as I sprint toward the one person who's never turned his back on me.

The lights are off at James's, but his treehouse is lit by a single beam of a flashlight peeking through the branches. I begin climbing my way up the creaky ladder. A moment later, I hear shuffling, and James sticks his head out, squinting in the dim light.

"Cassie?"

"Can I come in?" My voice cracks, and the look on his face softens immediately.

He reaches his hand out, his fingers warm and steady against my cold, trembling ones. Then, without a word, I wrap my arms around his chest and let myself breathe.

"It's okay. I've got you," he whispers, holding me close.

Something flutters in my chest. But in the back of my head, I hear a voice telling me I don't deserve this. I don't deserve him.

"I'm sorry for telling you to leave that night." I bite my lip, staring at the floor.

He stays quiet for a moment. "Cassie," he begins softly. "I know you've been through things you're not ready to talk about, and that's okay. But when you are ready... I'm here. I'll always be here."

I want to tell him the truth. I want to believe that someone could love the worst parts of me and still stay.

Instead, I lean forward, kissing him. He doesn't pull away, and when we part, I'm breathless.

And terrified. And hopeful.

I glance around the treehouse. The wooden walls are covered in concert posters, their colors faded from years of sunlight. There's a small armchair tucked into one corner, its cushions sagging, and a collection of old books piled up next to it.

Tacked onto a wooden beam is a Polaroid of a little girl with red hair, her nose sunburnt and peppered with freckles. For a moment, I wonder who she is. But I don't ask.

Slowly, I lean into him, my head finding its place on his chest. The steady rhythm of his heartbeat becomes a quiet lullaby in the silence. I close my eyes, and for the first time, I allow myself to let go. The fears, the doubts, the broken pieces of myself — they all begin to fade, and I finally find a moment of peace.

As the morning light seeps into the treehouse, I blink awake, feeling the warmth of James beside me. And then I realize—

It's morning.

I sit up quickly, shaking James awake. "James, wake up! We fell asleep!"

And then —

"James? Are you up there?" a voice calls from below, her tone light and playful.

He stirs awake, blinking in confusion as he registers the voice. "Oh shit," he mutters, scrambling to sit up. "Julie, wait!"

The treehouse door creaks open, and the girl pops her head in, eyes widening at the sight of us. She has James's chocolate brown eyes, his dark curly hair, and the same crooked grin.

"Didn't know you'd be hosting a sleepover up here," she teases.

"It wasn't a sleepover." His face flushes.

The girl raises an eyebrow, still playfully smirking.

"Just... don't say anything, okay?" James adds, his voice desperate. "Please don't tell Dad."

She pauses before relenting with a sigh, though her eyes are still gleaming with amusement. "Fine. But you owe me one."

"What are you even doing here?"

"It's spring break, dummy," she replies. "Which means you're stuck with me for the next week."

She starts to back down the ladder, then pauses, a mischievous grin on her face. Her eyes flick to me, then to James. Then, with a chuckle, she disappears down the ladder.

I glance at James, who's still red-faced.

He lets out a long sigh, shaking his head. "That's my sister, Julie."

I nudge him with my shoulder. "Could've been worse."

His eyes meet mine, and for a moment, we just sit there.

"So..." I start, breaking the silence, "What now?"

Standing and reaching his hand out to me, he says, "I guess... we could grab pancakes at Marg's?"

I take it, his fingers wrapping around mine as he pulls me to my feet.

As we walk together, I realize something's changed between us. Maybe it was always there, tucked quietly between us. But now, with the morning light warming our backs and our hands intertwined, it feels undeniable.

It feels real.

Chapter 13
for betty
James

I don't even know if she listens to tapes anymore.

The cassette tape spins. Rewinds. Stops. Spins again. The cassette clicks in the player like it's judging me. Which, fair. I've been sitting in this damn treehouse since sunrise, recording and rewinding like a lunatic.

Nothing sounds right. Nothing sounds enough. But somehow, every song is *her*. Every single one.

Track 1 is *Don't Stop Believin'* by Journey. I remember that night we sang it in my truck, windows down, laughing like idiots. That was the night I kissed her for the first time. When everything changed between us.

Track 3 is *Harvest Moon* by Neil Young — the song we slow-danced to at Sadie Hawkins last year. I wonder if she remembers. That moment. That song. That feeling between us.

Track 5 is *Linger* by The Cranberries. Betty used to hum it without realizing, half under her breath, usually while doodling little flowers in the margins of her notebook.

A Polaroid shifts slightly in the draft, pinned to the wooden beam above the window. It was Betty's seventh birthday. Her front teeth were missing, her hair a wild frizzy mess, the way it always was on a humid day. She's holding a toad in one hand and a juice box in the other.

I remember every birthday.

The one when she turned eleven and I gave her a rock shaped like a heart I found in the creek. The one when she turned fifteen and I saved up enough money to buy her a box of Laffy Taffy. She wasn't a big fan of the candy, but she liked to collect the wrappers for the little jokes. And last year on her sixteenth birthday, she sat on the hood of my truck and told me her favorite color was yellow because it reminds her of lightning bugs in the summer.

And next week she's turning seventeen. In a city I've never been to. With people I've never met. And I'm here, making a freaking mixtape for a girl I haven't seen since August. I don't even know if I want her to get this tape. I just... I want her to know I haven't forgotten. That I remember *everything*.

I eject the tape and lean back in my chair. The wood creaks under me. The same creak it made that night we came up here to watch the stars, and she brought hot chocolate in a thermos that leaked through her backpack.

The truth is, I miss Betty. It didn't hit me when I walked into school on the first day of junior year and passed by her old locker, though I did pause, just long enough to stare at the dent in the door where she slammed it shut too hard. It didn't hit me when I saw her name carved into the corner of the lunch table, right next to mine.

It hit me when I caught myself walking to the creek out of

habit like I'd find her sitting there on the log, chin propped in her hands, watching the tadpoles. It hit me at Marg's when Cassie and I were sitting at the corner booth, and *Linger* started playing. I didn't say anything. I just stared at the jukebox like it had betrayed me. Cassie kept talking, but all I could hear was Betty's voice, humming along.

It never hit me all at once. Missing her came in pieces — in the quiet, ordinary things. In places she touched without really meaning to. And maybe that's the part that messes with me the most. She's *everywhere*. Even when she's miles away.

I flip the cassette over in my hands. It's blank on one side. I pick up a marker and write — ***For Betty***.

I picture her opening it, maybe surrounded by new friends, humming some song I don't even know she loves yet. I picture her face — confused, then maybe... smiling.

The sky starts to darken — the last light catching the tops of the trees in gold. I walk down the ladder with the mixtape in my back pocket. For a moment, I consider just tossing it, letting the creek swallow it. Then I think about mailing it to her. But what if she's forgotten me already? What if she hates it? What if it just makes her sad?

My fingers fumble with the tape in my pocket. And for now, that's where it'll stay.

Chapter 14

seventeen

Betty

I gaze at my clock. Exactly three days, eleven hours, and forty-three minutes. The numbers tick away.

Staring down at my hands, they seem too small to be those of a girl who will enter the world as a seventeen-year-old in exactly three days, eleven hours, and forty-three minutes.

I hate birthdays. They mark the inevitability of change and the relentless passage of time; two things I loathe.

I'm still lost in thought when Mom calls from the kitchen. "Goose! Come out here quick."

Sitting on the kitchen table is a cake with pink frosting and cherries lining the top. The words, ***Happy Birthday, Betty*** are written out in vanilla icing between seventeen flickering candles.

I look at Mom, her hands clasp together in eagerness, then to Dad, his stern face manages to carve out a smile.

"My birthday isn't for another three days?"

"I know," Mom says, taking my hand and guiding me into the room. "But we have a surprise for you. First — blow out your candles and make a wish."

Closing my eyes, I blow out all seventeen candles in one breath, but I don't make a wish. I've stopped believing in that stuff — falling stars, four-leaf clovers, birthday candles. They don't make your dreams come true. They just make you hope for things that won't happen.

Mom places a small, square box in front of me — the kind you'd expect to hold earrings or something delicate.

I slip the lid off.

Inside, nestled on a bed of cotton, is an old brass key. It's scratched and a little tarnished, with a faded green ribbon looped through the top.

"I don't get it," I say, holding it up.

"It's a key to Grandma Martin's house," Mom says gently. "She's already set up the guest room for you."

I glance up at Mom, eyes wide.

"Goose," she begins, softer now, "we know how much Gallipolis means to you. And you're right — we should've talked to you before making such a big decision. So, we've decided, if that's where your heart is, then home is where you should be."

My throat tightens. I can't speak. I just stare at the key, my fingers curling around it. It's so simple. So small. But it means *everything*.

"It's already arranged," she adds. "Your flight leaves the first week of August. That gives you time to pack your things and tie up any loose ends before school begins."

"I'm going home?" I whisper the words like a secret. Like if I say them too loud, I'll jinx it.

Dad smiles. "Happy birthday, squirt." Then, with a playful glint in his eye, he adds, "Might be time to visit that bookshop of yours. Let Mr. McGregor know you won't be a regular much longer."

I smile, already reaching for my jacket. My eye catches my ring: bright green, the happiest color I've seen in months.

The cheerful chime of the bell greets me as I step into McGregor's Nook, just like it always does when the door swings open.

"Betty!" Mr. McGregor calls from atop a ladder, dusting the books on the shelves. "Back so soon?"

"I've got some news."

He pauses mid-swipe, then sets the rag aside and begins his slow climb down.

"I'm moving back home," I say, my smile slightly fading. "To Gallipolis."

"Well," he says, voice warm, "Gallipolis is lucky to have you back."

"I wanted to tell you how much I appreciate you," I continue, feeling my heart stutter. "You're one of the only friends I've made here, and I'm going to miss you."

Fitzgerald scampers out from behind the counter and leaps onto the desk, meowing indignantly.

"And Fitzgerald, of course."

Mr. McGregor places a gentle hand on my shoulder. "Of all

the customers who have wandered into my shop over the years, you've been my favorite."

He fumbles around in his pocket, pulling out his crimson lapel pin. "I want you to have this. You are a bright young girl, Betty, and I believe that you would do extraordinary things at Cornell University."

"Thank you, Mr. McGregor," I say, taking the pin.

"Don't be a stranger." His eyes crinkle with a smile. "Bookshops remember the ones who needed them most."

As I step back, I collide with Simon, sending a stack of books tumbling from his grasp. The sound of hardcovers thuds against the wooden floor. I quickly bend down to help him gather the scattered books.

"You've got quite the collection this week," I say, handing him the last book. "Reading anything good?"

Simon glances down. "Well, I just finished this one. It's about a magic school for wizards." He scratches the back of his neck. "Listen, I didn't mean to eavesdrop, but I overheard you talking. You're going home — back to Ohio?"

I nod. "I leave in a couple of months."

I want to tell him that I'll miss him. That part of me hopes our paths will cross again. But the words stay stuck in my throat.

"Oh, I almost forgot," he says, handing me a journal with a pink ribbon delicately tied around it. "This is for you."

My finger glides along the ribbon. It feels soft and familiar, like the one Mom used to tie in my hair.

"You mentioned your birthday was coming up, and I noticed your other one was nearly full." He smiles, his gaze meeting mine. "I hope this inspires you to keep writing, Betty. Your words deserve to be heard."

I half expect him to hug me or even lean in for a spur-of-the-moment kiss. But he doesn't. He just smiles, then turns on his heel and gives me a goodbye wave over his shoulder.

I take a slow glance around, letting everything sink in: the scent of worn pages, the endless rows of shelves crammed with stories that haven't been read, the overstuffed armchair tucked away in the corner.

As I turn to leave, uncertain if I'll ever be back, my throat tightens. Just three more months in New York. Three more weeks at St. Cecilia. Three more days until I turn seventeen.

Chapter 15
the fourth of july
James

The fireworks haven't started yet.

My eyes linger on the spot where Betty and I kissed last summer beneath the lights of the Ferris Wheel. We were sticky with sweat, our lips tasting like cherry soda. I remember handing her a plastic mood ring I'd won at the ring toss.

I wonder if she still has that ring.

The Fourth of July was always magic. Not the kind with wands and spells, but the kind that lives in the glow of sparklers and the sweetness of lemonade on a humid afternoon. For as long as I can remember, Betty and I spent it together. It started at the Gallia County fair, where we'd ride the Gravitron until one of us threw up... as if it was a contest.

But my favorite part?

That was later, when the sun dipped low and Betty and I climbed out of her bedroom window and onto the roof. We'd sit shoulder to shoulder, watching the fireworks burst overhead. She always brought Pop Rocks, and we'd dump the whole packet into our mouths at once, laughing at the way they fizzed on our tongues.

Now, standing at the Gallia County Fair, everything feels the same, but also not.

Lately, my thoughts keep circling back to Betty; what she's

doing, who she's with, and what's on her mind. I know I shouldn't be dwelling on it because it's not fair to Cassie, but it feels like I'm caught between two worlds, one foot stuck in the past and the other trying to move forward.

Cassie laces her fingers through mine, her laughter cutting through my thoughts as she tugs me toward the funhouse. The colorful lights flicker above as we step inside a kaleidoscope of distorted mirrors.

But then, I stop, tilting my head in one of the mirrors.

It's her freckled nose, her blue eyes, looking at me like she's right there, clear as day. I reach out, my hand grazing the glass. Of course, it's just my reflection, twisted and stretched, but for a minute, it felt real.

I tear my gaze away from the mirror, forcing my feet to move. I catch up to Cassie as she whirls out of the maze and into the open air. She pulls me toward a patch of grass, and we sit close, her head on my shoulder.

After a moment, Cassie cocks her head up at me. "Everything okay?"

I blink, shaking my head slightly. "Yeah. Just... thinking too much."

"About what?"

"Do you ever—" I begin, but my voice trails off.

"Do you ever... what?"

I sigh. "Do you ever feel homesick... for a memory?"

Cassie blinks. "Yeah," she says, her voice quieter now. "I think everyone does at some point. It's called nostalgia."

Her answer is simple, but it feels heavier than it should. She takes my hand, her thumb brushing over my knuckles.

"The thing is," she says after a moment, "memories are nice, but they're not where you're supposed to live."

She's right. I know she's right.

Cassie deserves all of me, not these cracked parts still haunted by someone else. But I can't stop wondering what I'd say if I ever saw Betty again. Because the truth is, no matter how bright the fireworks are, they don't feel the same without her.

Chapter 16
where the lilacs bloom
Betty

LaGuardia feels a lot bigger, like it's grown up since last August. Or maybe I'm just seeing it differently now. The taxi pulls up, and I grab my Care Bear suitcase, hooking my arm through Mom's. Dad takes the lead, weaving us through the crowds. By the time we reach Gate C24, I'm practically cutting off Mom's circulation.

"You've got your boarding pass?" Dad asks. Again. For maybe the fifth time.

"Yes," I say, holding it up like evidence.

He launches into logistics, ticking them off as if I don't already know the plan. "The Greyhound to Gallipolis leaves at 9:45 sharp. Don't miss it."

"I know, Dad," I mumble, clutching the pass a little tighter.

"And don't forget to call us when you land," Mom adds, resting a warm hand on my shoulder.

Dad pats my back. "Have a safe flight."

Mom pulls me into a hug, her handkerchief already out. "Our little Goose is all grown up."

As I walk down the jet bridge, I turn back one last time. Mom's dabbing at her eyes, and Dad's standing tall, like he's trying not to cry.

I slide into my window seat next to an older woman who

doesn't even glance up from her crossword puzzle. Staring out the window, I watch as the city shrinks below, skyscrapers swallowed up by clouds.

As the plane begins its descent, I prepare myself for the ambiguity of what lies ahead. During the bus ride to Gallipolis, my stomach twists in knots, either from nerves, motion sickness, or the lack of food in my stomach, or maybe a nauseating combination of all three.

When I step off the bus, I already see Grandma, waving her arms eagerly. She's wearing her yellow sundress, the one she made herself, and a big floppy hat to match. I run to her, dropping my suitcase and throwing myself into her arms. Nestling my face into the crook of her shoulder, I draw in a deep breath, savoring the delicate scent of her honeysuckle perfume.

She squeezes me tight, then pulls back to get a good look at me. "You've grown."

After dropping my suitcase in the trunk of the Buick LeSabre, I join Grandma in the front, taking in the scenes out the window as they pass by in a blur.

We pull up to the Victorian house on Maple Avenue, everything just as I remember: the creaky porch, the lopsided mailbox. The lilacs are gone now, but I can still picture them in the corner by the steps, where they used to bloom every spring.

With a turn of the key, Grandma opens the wooden door.

The creak of the floorboards beneath my feet echoes through the foyer as I run my fingers along the dusty banister. Sunlight streams in through stained glass windows, casting vibrant hues of emerald and sapphire across the intricate wallpaper. Portraits of my stern-faced ancestors look down at me from their frames, their eyes seemingly following my every move with silent scrutiny.

I make my way up the staircase and push open the door to my bedroom. The room is bathed in a soft, golden light filtering through the lace curtains draped over the tall windows. A large, four-poster bed sits in the middle of the room, its mahogany frame reaching toward the ceiling. I fall backwards onto the bed, sinking into the floral quilt.

Then, I hear a soft knock on my door. Grandma peeks her head through the doorway with a smile.

"How are you getting settled?"

"Just taking it all in," I say, sitting up.

She steps into the room. "I've got fresh lemonade waiting."

I follow her downstairs and take a seat at the table.

"So," she begins, settling into the chair across from me. "Tell me about New York."

"New York," I echo with a slight smile. "There were good and bad parts, but I think, in the end, the good outweighed the bad."

She leans forward, her eyes lighting up.

"The bad parts were being away from home." I pause. "I missed you and —"

"James?" she blurts cheerfully.

I shift in my seat. "Yeah, a little." But the words feel untrue. It was more than just a little.

She leans in closer, her voice softening. "Have you heard from him?"

"Not since last fall," I answer, doodling in the condensation on my glass.

I wonder how much James has changed since I last saw him. Has he gotten taller? Is his hair longer? Does he still smell like pine needles and cinnamon gum? Has his voice changed? Is it deeper now?

She watches me for a moment, then places a gentle hand on my leg. "Sometimes coming home takes a little while to feel right again."

I nod, my throat tightening.

She gives me a knowing look before getting up, leaving me alone with my thoughts. The lemonade glass sweats in my palm. I stare at the condensation, tracing lazy circles, wondering —

What will happen when I see James again?

Chapter 17
Cardigan
James

My shift at Al's ran long, and my head's still spinning with inventory counts. The bell over the door jingles as Cassie and I step into Marg's Diner. Her fingers are laced with mine, tugging me toward our booth, the one tucked in the corner.

I glance up, and then I see her.

She's sitting in our booth, her head bent over a menu she doesn't even need. Beside the menu, a straw wrapper is twisted into a tight knot just like she always used to do. She's wearing my cardigan. The one I gave her the night before she left. The one I thought I'd never see again.

She looks up, and for a split second, her eyes catch mine. The clatter of dishes, Dolly's raspy voice calling out orders, and Cassie's soft fingers wrapped around mine all suddenly fade away. Because Betty's right there, in the last place I expected her to be. And even though I told myself that I've moved on, it feels like someone just yanked the rug out from under me.

"James?" Cassie's voice cuts through the haze. She's looking at me, her brow furrowed like she can't quite figure out what just happened. "You look like you've seen a ghost."

I hesitate. My feet feel heavy, like they're caught in the diner's sticky tile. I shouldn't leave Cassie like this, but before I can stop myself, I let go of her hand and start walking to Betty.

Chapter 18
The One
Betty

I glare at her. Short, blonde, perfect. Like a Barbie doll come to life. And then I see her hand, her fingers intertwined around James's like he belongs to her. Like it's normal. Like it's always been this way.

He lets go of her hand, as if that changes what I saw.

"Betty?" His voice catches, and he's walking toward me, the blonde girl trailing closely behind, clearly dumbfounded. "—Uh, when did you get back into town?"

"A few days ago." I grip the menu to steady myself, my knuckles white.

"This is—" He pauses, gesturing toward her. "This is Cassie Parker."

I don't remember standing, but I'm on my feet, face-to-face with him. Then, I shove past and head straight for the door.

His voice rings out behind me, and it's enough to make me falter, but I don't stop. Not until I'm outside, fumbling with the kickstand of my bike like it's the only thing tethering me to reality.

Before I know it, his hands clamp down on my handlebars, holding me in place. "Can we please just talk about this?"

I freeze, breath catching. "What is there to talk about?"

His gaze drops to a cigarette butt on the ground.

"Do you—" I hesitate. I hate that I did, like I'm scared to hear his answer. "Do you love her?"

His eyes widen as if I've slapped him.

"Do you love her?" I ask again, my voice cracking this time.

He looks so defeated, so unlike the James I've known my whole life. He wants to say something, I can see it in his face, but whatever words he's searching for just aren't there.

"Betty I—" James runs a hand through his hair. "You were gone. I didn't know if—"

"If what?" I cut him off. "If I still cared? If you still mattered to me? God, I—" My voice breaks, and with a shake of my head, I turn away.

He steps forward. "I-I made you a mixtape... for your birthday. I was going to send it to you, but—"

"Yeah?" I laugh bitterly, shaking my head. "Why don't you take that mixtape and shove it up your—"

"Stop," he interrupts, his voice sharp.

He looks at me, and for a split second, I see the James I used to know. The boy who swore we'd be best friends forever. But then it's gone, slipping away as quickly as it came.

"You were the one person, James... the *one* person I thought would never hurt me." I want to scream it — throw it at him like glass — but all I can do is whisper, "But I was wrong."

I don't wait for his response. I hop on my bike and pedal

away, the wind whipping at my face and the tears blurring my vision. Behind me, I hear him shout my name once, maybe twice. But I don't stop. I don't look back.

Chapter 19
Ghost
Cassie

I watch James enter the diner again, hands shoved into his pockets, his eyes avoiding mine. He sits across from me, picking up the menu, pretending like whatever just happened... didn't happen.

"James," I say hesitantly. "Who was that?"

His eyes flick up from the menu for a moment, but they dart away too quickly. "That was Betty," he says, shifting in his seat. "We grew up right across the street from each other."

The way he says it feels off, like he's tiptoeing around the truth, afraid of revealing too much. I wait for more, but he doesn't say anything else.

"Why was she upset?"

He sighs, dropping the menu onto the table. "Last summer, things between us... changed," he says, his voice tight. "We ended up becoming more than friends. But then she moved away with her parents. We tried to make it work, but... it just didn't."

There it is. The hesitation. The way he overemphasized the word "tried."

He reaches across the table and takes my hand, holding it with a grip that's almost too tight. I can feel the way his fingers tremble ever-so-slightly. I don't think he even knows it.

I want to say something, but before I can respond, Dolly walks over with a mug of coffee, setting it down between us with a cheery smile.

"James, did you hear? Betty's back in town," she says, like it's just another piece of gossip.

Dolly walks away, but her words ring in my ears, louder than anything else in the diner.

"Do you still have feelings for her?" My voice comes out quieter than I mean it to, but I see the way his body stiffens, like I've hit a nerve.

His eyes drop to the table, avoiding my gaze. "No, I—" He cuts himself off and looks up at me. "I've known Betty for a really long time. But those feelings—they're not like they were, Cass. I swear."

I nod, even though a part of me is still uncertain. I want to believe him, but the way he keeps pulling away, distancing himself... it's enough to plant a seed of doubt.

Something else tugs at the back of my mind, something about Betty's face. Her eyes looked sad. Hurt, even. And suddenly, I wish I'd followed her. To tell her I'm sorry, even though I'm not entirely sure what for.

"I..." I swallow, the lie already forming. "I just remembered... I have some chores back at home." I stand up, forcing a smile, though I know it doesn't reach my eyes.

James doesn't say anything else. He just sits there, eyes

still fixed on the twisted straw wrapper. Part of me hopes he'll follow, chase me outside just like he did with Betty.

But part of me knows he won't.

Chapter 20
Cough Syrup
Betty

I'm cross-legged on my bedroom floor, surrounded by Grandma's old makeup bags. The zipper on one is broken, gaping open like a secret spilling out. When I was little, I'd watch her dab powder on her cheeks in delicate strokes.

She used to say, "A touch of color, Betty, and you can brighten up the gloomiest day."

I reach for the blush, swirling the bristles in the compact, then dusting it over my cheeks. It smells faintly like roses. In the mirror, the color blooms against my pale skin.

Then, I pick up a tube of pink lipstick, rolling it up. The edges are smudged, the tip flattened from years of use. I lean close to the mirror and swipe it across my lips. The color is brighter than I'm used to, definitely not my usual Lip Smacker.

I study my reflection, tilting my face, hoping the angle might change something. But the mirror just stares back, plain and unkind. My face is unremarkable, too easy to overlook. No amount of lipstick or blush will change that. I run a hand through my hair, sighing.

Not prettier. Just better disguised.

By the time I arrive at Nina's party, it's already loud, the bass rattles in my ribcage. I head straight to the punch bowl, the floor sticky from one too many spilled drinks, and pour myself a cup. Too bitter. Like cough syrup. I drink it anyway.

Just as I'm about to step away, someone slams into me from behind.

"Seriously?" I snap, spinning around to glare at the careless person.

Of course, it's Donnie.

Donnie Pilgrim has been in my life longer than I care to admit. Preschool, kindergarten, middle school. Same classrooms. Same playgrounds. Same dorky bowl cut. He was always there, hovering like a moth to a porch light, laughing too loudly and quoting Hitchcock too many times.

"I-I didn't mean to," he stammers, voice cracking slightly. "Someone knocked into me. I swear."

His eyes are wide, his cup tilted sideways in one hand, a blotchy stain already blooming on his polo. His glasses sit slightly askew on his nose, his crooked grin apologetic. He bolts to the punch bowl and returns with a fresh cup, holding it out like an olive branch.

I stare at the cup, then at him. His ears are bright red.

"Y'know we missed you last year," he says, rubbing the back of his neck like he doesn't know what to do with his hands. "Holy shit, I just remembered — you missed when the school almost burnt down last spring! Some freshman microwaved his foil-wrapped burrito and shorted the power in the whole east wing. The fire department had to come!"

I blink.

"Honestly?" He shrugs. "It was the most hopeful day of the entire school year."

I give him a look sharp enough to cut through his rambling. Part of me knows he means well, he always does, but another part of me is too tired to deal with his endless stream of chatter. I turn the other direction, and then I see them.

James and Cassie, tucked into the corner by the window, their heads tilted together. She's saying something, and he's laughing, his whole face lighting up the way it used to with me.

My hand grips the cup so tightly that the plastic bends, the liquid inside sloshing against my knuckles.

Then James reaches out, brushing a strand of her hair back. Before I can stop myself, I gulp the punch down, ignoring the burn coursing down my throat.

When I glance back at them, he's kissing her.

My hand shakes as I pour another drink, the cup trembling like it knows I shouldn't. I gulp it down anyway.

With my vision blurring, I let my eyes wander the room, and they land on Miles. He's grinning, holding up his hands in victory at the beer pong table.

Miles Cooper is always the loudest in the room — the unofficial class clown. In seventh grade, he told all the boys I had mosquito bite boobs. The worst part? James is friends with him. It doesn't make sense to me since they are practically opposites — but James always sees things in people that I miss. And maybe Miles has grown past the dumb middle school punchlines. At least my boobs have grown since then.

And then, an idea forms in my mind. It's reckless and stupid, but I stumble over to him anyway. Heart pounding, my brain is screaming at me to stop, to think, but I don't.

"Kiss me," I say, the heat rushing to my cheeks.

I don't wait for his response. With trembling hands, I grab his face and press my lips to his. His mouth is wet and sloppy, but I don't pull away.

His friends erupt into cheers and whistles, their laughter and high-fives ringing out like he's just won the state championship.

When we break apart, Miles blinks, a slow grin spreading across his face. "Damn, Thompson," he says, his voice laced with disbelief. "Didn't know you had that in you."

My eyes return to the spot where James and Cassie were standing. I wanted him to see. I wanted him to feel the same hurt I felt when he kissed her. But he's gone, and for a moment, I wonder if he even saw me.

If he cared.

"Let's get out of here," Miles says, grabbing my hand before I can process his words.

He pulls me toward the stairs, weaving through the crowd as my legs stumble to keep up. As we climb, my steps become clumsy, my knees wobbling beneath me. The room spins slightly, colors and faces blurring. I want to stop, to ask him where we're going, but my lips won't move, and my feet follow on their own.

Chapter 21
Something is Very Wrong
Cassie

The music is too loud, it drums through me like a steady heartbeat. I scan the crowd looking for James. Something is off about him tonight.

Then, out of the corner of my eye, I spot Betty, her body slumped against Miles as they make their way up the stairs. His arm is snaked around her waist, and she's leaning into him, limp like a rag doll.

A cold shiver runs down my spine as I watch them disappear behind a door. Before I know it, my feet begin to move, my instincts screaming at me that something isn't right.

That something is very wrong.

My hands tremble as I reach the top of the stairs. I twist the doorknob and shove it open. Miles is on the bed, pinning Betty down. His mouth is on hers, but she's crying. Pleading. Her voice is small and broken.

I storm into the room. Miles barely turns his head before I shove him away from Betty. He stumbles back, his curse slurring as he catches himself against the nightstand.

"What the hell is wrong with you?!" My voice shakes as I step between them.

Miles stares at me, stunned for a moment. Then, he scoffs, rolling his eyes. "Jesus," he slurs, running a hand through his hair. "We were just having a little fun." He reaches for his drink, completely unbothered. "Didn't realize you were such a prude."

"Get out," I growl, stepping toward him.

He pushes past, the stench of beer clinging to his breath. Then he disappears down the hall.

I turn to Betty, grabbing her arm and pulling her up. She's unsteady on her feet, her legs wobbling like they might give out at any moment, but I hold her tight. We move down the stairs, out the door, and into the night.

Betty stumbles, her body heavy against mine, as I guide her to the curb. She collapses there, her head hanging low. Suddenly, she lurches forward, her whole body trembling as she vomits on the pavement.

"It's okay," I say, holding her hair back. "You're okay."

She leans against the streetlight, her body shaking with every breath. Her eyes are red, her face ghostly pale, and when she looks at me, there's something desperate behind her eyes.

"Don't tell James about this."

I stare at her, my throat tightening.

"Please." She grabs my arm, her fingers digging into my wrist. "Swear you won't tell him."

"I promise."

She lets out a shaky breath and stands. "I can get myself home."

"Wait—"

But she's already walking, her steps uneven as she moves down the street. I watch her go, her silhouette shrinking until it disappears into the darkness.

My stomach twists, memories flashing through my mind of all the times I saw someone hurting and chose to look away, of all the times I chose silence instead of stepping in.

But not tonight.

Chapter 22
What Would Mom Say?

James

The door creaks open as I step inside, my eyes scanning the dim living room. The air feels heavier, like I can't quite catch my breath. Julie steps into the hallway, her brows furrowing when she sees me.

She takes a step closer, her eyes searching mine. "You okay?"

I shrug, running a hand through my hair. I shouldn't care. I shouldn't even be thinking about it. Then, it spills out. "I saw Betty at the party. Kissing Miles."

The words feel jagged in my throat, like they're cutting on the way out. The image of Betty and Miles — their lips locked, her hand on his chest — replays in my mind, seared into my brain.

Julie watches me for a second, her expression softening. "I thought you went to the party with Cassie?"

"I did." I look away, feeling guilt creep up my spine. "But I... I left her there."

"You left her?"

I nod, the knot in my chest loosening just enough to take a shaky breath.

She sighs. "Dad's working late again. There's lasagna in the fridge if you're hungry."

But before I can answer, something clicks in my brain. "Jules, what are you doing here? Didn't your semester start?"

She leans against the counter. "Yeah, it did."

I shift my weight from one foot to the other, trying to gauge her mood. "So, what? You just decided not to go back?"

She shrugs.

I take a step closer, studying her. Julie, my annoyingly smart, straight-A sister, suddenly unsure.

Julie exhales, her shoulders sagging. "I don't know what I want anymore." Her voice is small, quieter than I'm used to hearing. "Everything about my life suddenly feels... wrong." She looks down at her hands, fiddling with the sleeve of her sweater, before looking up, her eyes glistening."I just... I need time. A semester off. To figure things out."

I nod, leaning against the fridge. "Then do it."

Julie lets out a slight chuckle, her shoulders relaxing a bit.

"Jules, you're the smartest person I know," I continue. "You'll figure it out. You always do."

We're quiet for a moment. Then, Julie breaks the silence.

"Okay, here's the deal," she says, crossing her arms. "I'll figure out my college situation." She points a finger at me. "You figure out your love life."

"How?" I raise an eyebrow.

"Talk to Betty," she continues, nudging my arm. "You guys have been best friends since you were practically in diapers."

"I don't know, Jules." I sigh. "I doubt she wants to look at me, let alone talk."

Julie raises an eyebrow, clearly unconvinced. "Just try."

"I did," I say, slumping back. "And she ran away... crying."

Julie exhales. "Okay, but did you actually *talk* to her?"

I shoot her a look. "What do you mean?"

"What did you say to her?"

I hesitate, thinking back to the look on her face, the way she turned and bolted before I could even find the words I wanted to say.

"I-I don't know." I shrug. "I barely got a chance to say anything."

Julie groans. "Well, there's your problem, James. You need to actually say something. Like, full sentences. With words."

"And what if she doesn't want to hear them?"

Julie gives me a look, the kind that says I'm being an idiot. "She does. This is Betty we're talking about — the girl who used to make mud pies with you in the backyard."

I exhale, rubbing my hands over my face. "How are you so good at this? Knowing exactly what to say?"

Julie smirks. "Because Mom gave me this exact talk when I had two guys chasing me."

For the first time all night, the heaviness in my chest lifts, just a little. Maybe we're both a little lost right now. But at least we've got each other.

Chapter 23
The Next Morning
Cassie

I knock on James's door, my heart thudding a little harder than I expect. It's stupid. But how can I act normal, like everything is fine, after last night? Because I'm not fine. I'm anything but fine.

Betty's words echo in my mind, a silent reminder of what I witnessed, no... what I experienced last night. Seeing Miles on top of her. Screaming at him. Holding her hair back. Promising I won't tell James. All while James was missing.

When he opens it, his face shifts from looking happy to see me to instant regret. "Shit, I-I'm really sorry... about last night," he says, like he's practiced it a hundred times.

"Where did you go?" I ask, taking a seat on the porch step.

He sits down next to me, just far enough that we're not touching. "I just... I wasn't feeling good," he says, avoiding my eyes. "I'm sorry I left you so abruptly."

"It's fine... can I ask you something?" My gaze drifts out toward the driveway, lingering on his rusted truck. "Do you know where Betty lives?" The words come out faster than I planned, too sharp to sound casual.

He hesitates. "Yeah, I heard that she's living with her grandma." His brows furrow, clearly confused. "Why?"

I pause, scrambling for an excuse. "She left her wallet at

the party," I lie, forcing a smile. "I want to return it."

"That's really nice of you, Cassie." He looks at me for a moment longer. Finally, he says, "It's the Victorian house on Maple. You can't miss it."

As I stand to leave, his voice stops me. "Cassie, is everything okay?"

No. Everything is not okay.

I force a smile, shrugging. "Yeah, why wouldn't it be?"

Walking down the sidewalk, I feel his eyes on me, like he's waiting for me to turn around. When I round the corner, I exhale and let my shoulders drop.

The Victorian house on Maple Avenue looms over me. I take a deep breath and knock three times, my heart pounding with every echoing thud. The door creaks open, and a kind-faced woman greets me. Her silver hair is swept into a bun, and her voice is warm like honey.

"Can I help you?"

"Hi, I'm Cassie. I-I'm a friend... of Betty's," I say, glancing past her into the house.

Her face brightens. "Well, aren't you sweet? Come on in."

The house is quiet except for the hum of a radio in the kitchen. It feels like a postcard, all polished wood and framed family portraits.

"She's upstairs, second door on the left."

I climb the staircase, the wood creaking underneath my

weight. When I reach Betty's door, I knock lightly. There's a long pause, and then the door opens just enough for her face to peek out. Her eyes are red-rimmed, her hair in messy knots.

"What are you doing here?"

"Your grandma let me in," I say, leaning against the frame.

She hesitates, then opens the door. Her eyes flick toward the hallway, like she's already regretting it.

Her cardigan, the one she wore that day at Marg's, is folded neatly at the edge of her bed, like she doesn't want it to wrinkle. Her blankets are twisted, draped off the mattress. A glass of water sits on the nightstand. Next to it, a crumpled tissue.

"Betty," I say, stepping into the room. "I wanted to make sure you're okay."

She stares at me. "Why? It's not like we're friends."

"I know," I say, heart racing. "But I still care."

"I'm fine," she says, sinking onto her bed. Her tone is clipped, like she's trying to convince herself as much as me.

I take a step closer. "Betty, what happened to you last night isn't fine."

She looks away, jaw tightening. "You didn't tell James, did you?"

"No," I say, quietly. "I wouldn't do that to you."

She leans against her pillow, her body stiffening. "You should go."

"Betty —"

"Just go." Her voice cracks a little.

I turn to leave, her words echoing in my mind. I want to tell James... to share this weight so I'm not carrying it alone. But I promised her. And I don't know if I'll ever forget that look on her face when she made me swear.

Chapter 24
When a Tree Falls in a Forest
Betty

It's been one week since Nina's party, and it's been two days since I had my last nightmare. I tell myself that I'm fine, that I'm over it. But every time I close my eyes, he's still there; his breath, heavy and hot, so close to my ear. His hand, slick with sweat, digging into my thigh.

I don't tell anyone. Because if no one sees you hurting, are you even hurting? Kind of like the tree falling in the forest. Does it make a sound?

The bell rings, jarring me back. First day of senior year.

I slip my chunky headphones over my ears, Alanis Morrisette turned up just loud enough to drown out the noise around me. I find my locker and lean against it, watching the students walk by, all of them familiar, but also different.

"Betty."

I don't have to look up to know it's James. I tug off my headphones, letting them rest around my neck.

"I've been wanting to talk to you—" He stops, his eyes scanning me like he's piecing something together. "What's wrong?"

He's so good at reading me. Too good.

"Nothing. I'm fine."

"Something's wrong, Betty. I know you."

"I'm fine," I repeat, but it feels wrong. Like I'm lying to him. I hate lying to him.

"Talk to me," he says, leaning a little closer.

"Just leave me alone." I don't mean it. I want him here, but I shake my head, tears threatening to spill.

The hallway clears out as the next bell rings. Everyone's gone except us. He's still watching me, waiting.

"Do you... do you want to get out of here?" he asks, reaching his hand out to me.

I take it. Together, we walk out the door, our footsteps the only sound between us as we make our way to the creek. The water is low, barely a trickle over the rocks. I sit on a log, letting my bag drop to the ground with a soft thud.

James breaks the silence. "Look, I get it," he starts, leaning against a tree. "I'm probably the last person you want to talk to. But come on, Betty. You're my best friend, and I know something is bothering you."

"Like the obvious thing that's been bothering me for weeks?" I mutter weakly.

"No, it's something else," he replies, searching my eyes.

The words are stuck somewhere between my ribs, pressing against my lungs. The weight of everything I've been holding crashes down on me like a heavy anvil.

"I... I don't know how it happened," I stammer, my voice breaking with every breath. "He... he took me upstairs."

His gaze sharpens.

"And then suddenly he was —" My voice catches. I can't finish that sentence. I turn away, tears blurring my vision. "I told him to stop. I swear I told him."

The air between us goes still.

"Who?" His voice is barely above a whisper.

I swallow hard.

"Betty, who did this to you?" he asks again, this time more afraid.

I don't want to say it. I don't want to tell him it was Miles. But his name spills out before I can stop it.

James stiffens, fists curling at his sides.

"I shouldn't have kissed him," I quickly add, my voice shaking. "I should've known better. I—"

"No." James's voice is low, strained. "Don't do that. Don't blame yourself."

I shake my head, tears burning my eyes. "I shouldn't have gone to Nina's stupid party."

"Stop," he says, kneeling in front of me. "Betty, listen to me. None of this is your fault."

James wraps his arms around me, holding me close. I press my face into the crook of his shoulder. A sense of comfort I haven't felt in what feels like forever overcomes me. His touch, the scent of his hoodie, the warmth of his embrace.

It feels like home.

He doesn't say a word, just tightens his hold around me. We stay like that for a while, the sound of the creek filling the silence between us.

When I finally pull back, he looks at me. There's something behind his gaze, something dark, and yet uncertain, like a thought that's just surfaced, but he doesn't voice it. At least not immediately.

"Why didn't you tell me?"

"I... I couldn't." I wipe my face with the sleeve of my cardigan. "James, he's your friend."

"He's not anymore." His face hardens, and then he shakes his head, frustration lining his voice. "You shouldn't have carried this alone for so long. We used to tell each other everything."

"I know," I say, my voice catching. "I'm sorry."

"You have nothing to be sorry for." He exhales, rubbing the back of his neck. "I'm sorry if I made you feel like you couldn't talk to me." His gaze flickers to the ground for a second before returning to mine. "I never wanted to hurt you or for you to find out the way you—"

"James," I interject. "We don't have to talk about it."

"I want to." His voice is firmer now, insistent. "I need to know what happened between us. I-I mean, I wrote to you every week, and then your letters... they just stopped. I thought you were done with me."

"I thought the same about you," I admit, my voice cracking. "I waited. Weeks, months... but nothing came." I pause, wiping a tear from my eye. "But James, I never stopped writing, never stopped hoping. Up until I saw you in the diner with—" I hesitate, the words catching in my throat. "With her."

"Then what happened?" His voice is quieter now. Confused. Almost hurt.

"I don't know, James. But it doesn't matter anymore." I swallow hard. "You're with Cassie," I continue, forcing myself to say it, to acknowledge the reality. "And I'm just trying to get through the day."

We sit in silence for the rest of the afternoon, and for the first time in weeks, I feel like I can breathe again.

Chapter 25
Mascots & Polaroids
James

I'm not really paying attention to the homecoming game. Camera in hand, my eyes are scanning the sea of faces, looking for something to capture for the yearbook.

And then I see her.

Betty's sitting alone in the top row of the bleachers, her back against the railing, legs stretched out in front of her. Without thinking, I lift my camera and snap her picture, the sound of the shutter barely noticeable over the cheers as our team scores.

I make my way up the bleachers, the steps creaking under my feet. When I sit down beside her, she doesn't even look up. Her eyes are glued to the field, like she's enamored with the game, even though I know she's not.

"Hey," I say, trying to keep my voice light.

Betty glances at me, offering a faint smile.

We haven't talked since that day at the creek, so I'm not sure where we stand, exactly.

I shift on the bleacher, staring down at my sneakers before forcing the words out. "Are you going to the dance tomorrow?"

Betty hesitates for a moment, her fingers drumming on the bottle of root beer before she takes a quick swig.

"You could—" I pause, second-guessing myself. "I mean, if

you wanted to—" I should stop. I should leave it alone, drop it. "You could come with Cassie and me."

The second I say it, I regret it. I can already hear Julie saying, "Are you an idiot? Why would you ask your ex-girlfriend to go to a dance with you and your *current* girlfriend? Think James. Use your brain."

And honestly, I'd probably just nod and agree with her.

Betty's head snaps toward me, eyes burning. "I think I'd rather eat glass."

I barely have time to react before she's on her feet, disappearing into the crowd. I quickly stand, wanting to follow her, to tell her I'm sorry, but as soon as I take a step, I stop myself.

"Hey, James," Donnie says, pulling off the wolverine mascot head, his face flushed from the heat. "What are you doing up here all alone?"

"Well, I was up here with Betty," I say, sitting down in defeat. "But she took off."

Donnie scrunches his face and plops down beside me. "Yeah, what's going on with her? She seems off."

"She's just figuring some stuff out," I mutter, my eyes following the crowd below.

Donnie shifts, stretching his legs out in front of him. "Are you going to the dance tomorrow?"

"Yep," I mumble absentmindedly.

"I asked Nina Carmichael," Donnie begins casually, "but she turned me down. Said she's going with Miles Cooper."

My stomach tightens at the mere mention of his name.

"So I guess I'll just go solo this year," Donnie adds, giving me a playful nudge. "Should be fun."

I let out a snort. "You're not gonna spike the punch again, are you?"

He smirks. "Please. I have standards now."

"Well, Donnie, it was great catching up with you, but I'm going to head out," I say, standing and leaving the bleachers.

As I pass behind the stands, I see Miles leaning against the back wall, a cigarette dangling from his lips. The moment his eyes lock on mine, my fists clench.

"Hey, Cohen!"

I don't stop walking, but I slow just enough to acknowledge him.

"What's up, man?" he says, jogging to catch up.

My jaw tightens. "Just remembered I have some homework to finish up."

"Homework?" Miles squints, a grin tugging at the corner of his lips. "Dude, it's Friday night." He chuckles, stepping forward. "Everything good with your lady?"

"Cassie?" I raise an eyebrow. "Yeah, why?"

He laughs, shaking his head. "I meant Betty."

I freeze. "What about her?"

He shrugs. "Did you two have some kind of falling out?"

I don't answer.

"I mean, you know how it is with girls," he continues. "They get all moody and shit." Then he drops his cigarette, grinding it under his heel.

"I guess," I say through gritted teeth, turning away.

I hear sneakers scuff the pavement behind me. Donnie jogs up, slightly out of breath, tripping over his own feet.

"James, you forgot your camera," he says, holding it out. "Left it on the bleachers."

"Thanks," I mutter, slinging the strap over my shoulder.

He doesn't move. He just looks at me.

"You okay?" His eyes flick to my clenched fists. "You're scaring me a little. You look like you're ready to hit someone."

"I'm fine," I say too quickly.

But part of me wants to tell him.

About Betty. About Miles.

About why I look like I'm ready to hit someone.

Miles calls after us. "Hey, Donnie, if you're done holding hands with James, you should get back to prancing around in that mascot costume."

"Funny," Donnie mutters, just loud enough for Miles to hear, "coming from the guy who prances around in spandex on the lacrosse field."

I glance sideways just enough to see Donnie, chin lifted, his hands slightly trembling. With a shake of my head, I suppress a laugh and keep walking, fists buried in my pockets.

Chapter 26
The Dance
Betty

I stand in front of the mirror, the fabric of my dress rubbing against my skin like sand. I fidget with the straps, trying to make it fit just right.

"Don't you look pretty," Grandma says, stepping into the doorframe.

She insisted I go to the homecoming dance.

"You're young," she told me, pulling out a blue gown from a trunk in the attic. "You don't want to look back and wish you'd gone."

"I don't know, Grandma. I don't even have a date."

"Go for yourself, not for a boy." She said with a grin. "But if James happens to be there... well, you never know."

Of course, she would say that. She always brings up James, as if she knows I'll always have a soft spot for him.

I walk into the gym, my heart hammering against my chest like the bass of the music. The room is full of people talking in little clusters. Bodies moving too close. I clutch my necklace, like it's a lifeline.

I look at the door, plotting my escape, but just as I'm about to slip out, I see him, weaving through the crowd toward me.

"You look nice." Miles's eyes roam over me in a way that makes my skin crawl.

"I was just about to leave," I say, my fingers digging into the hem of my dress.

"Don't go yet." He steps closer, too close. "We should dance." He grabs my hands, pulling me toward the center of the gymnasium.

Something inside me jolts, like I'm back there, the night of the party, and my breath comes quicker.

I shake my head, pulling away. "I... I can't."

Miles clicks his tongue like he's disappointed in me. "Fine. Your loss."

I feel the eyes of others on me, like little daggers on the back of my neck. Suddenly, I can't catch my breath. I turn and push through the gym, desperate for air. Desperate to escape.

I step outside, feeling the ground shake beneath my feet. I collapse against the wall, my hands quivering. Tears prick at the corners of my eyes.

And then —

"Betty?" Donnie's voice breaks through the haze, but it feels distant, like he's calling from miles away. "Are you okay?"

I shake my head, my breath sharp and shallow.

"Betty, look at me," he says urgently, crouching down beside me. "Just focus on your breathing, okay?"

I close my eyes, tears spilling down my cheeks as the panic crashes over me, as if it might swallow me whole until I can't breathe, can't think, can't do anything but feel it.

"What... what's happening to me?" I manage to choke out.

"You're having a panic attack," Donnie says gently, his hand reaching out to steady me. "Just breathe, okay?"

And slowly, almost imperceptibly, the panic begins to retreat. My breath starts to slow, and the world feels less dizzying. My hands are still trembling, but the ground feels a little more stable under me.

"I'm sorry," I mutter softly, wiping the tears from my cheeks.

"Don't be," Donnie replies. "I used to get them a lot as a kid. They aren't fun." He offers me his hand. "Let me walk you home."

For a second, I hesitate, glancing around the empty parking lot, the music blaring from the gymnasium door behind me. I should be fine. I can walk myself home. But then I look at Donnie, and I know, deep down, I don't want to walk alone tonight. I take his hand, my fingers trembling as he pulls me to my feet.

Together, we walk toward the empty street.

After a while, Donnie looks at me. "Look, I'm not going to pretend I know what's going on with you lately. But I notice things, Betty. I notice you."

I don't say anything. I keep my focus on the sidewalk in front of me.

"Back at the dance, when Miles came up to you—" He

pauses, like he's searching for the right words. "You didn't look annoyed. Or even angry. You looked scared." He swallows, then adds, "Did something happen to you?"

My head snaps toward him. "Why? What do you know?"

"Nothing," he says quickly, holding his hands up. "I swear."

I nod once. "Good."

We walk a few more steps before he speaks again.

"I just... I know I would have wanted someone to help me through my panic attacks. Maybe if someone had noticed back then, things would be different."

I stop in my tracks. "I don't need you to feel sorry for me, and I definitely don't need you to save me."

"I'm sorry." He blinks. "We don't have to talk about it."

I exhale a shaky breath and start walking again, faster this time. He catches up but doesn't say anything else. We walk the rest of the way in silence. And even though I won't say it out loud to him, I'm grateful he stayed. That he didn't turn back. That he walked me home.

Chapter 27
Ivy
Cassie

My fingers fumble with the zipper.

Mom would know exactly which shade of lipstick would complement the lavender in my dress. Dad would probably peek in, tell me I looked beautiful, and then crack some half-hearted joke about curfews.

There's a knock at the door.

I take a deep breath and open it. James is standing there, one hand in his pocket while the other holds a white box. His tie is slightly crooked, and his hair looks like he's run his fingers through it a million times.

"You look beautiful." Then, he shifts his weight, glancing down at the box in his hand. "Here," he says, holding it out to me. "Figured this would go with your dress."

I open the box, revealing a delicate corsage of white roses and baby's breath. "Thank you," I say softly.

He shrugs. "It's no big deal."

We stand there for a moment, then he clears his throat. "You know, we don't have to go... to the dance, I mean."

I blink. "What?"

"We could skip it." A small smile tugs at the corner of his mouth. "These school dances are kind of lame anyway. We could do something else. Just you and me."

I stare at him for a moment and then nod. Because it's James, and somehow, he always knows exactly what to say to make me feel better.

With a smile, I follow him out the door.

James's truck rumbles down the back roads until we're parked in an open field, the truck's headlights casting long shadows over the grass. He hops out first, then comes around to open my door. It's sweet, in that effortless James way.

We climb into the bed of his truck, lying side by side on an old quilt he pulls from behind the seat. For a while, we just listen. To the crickets. The wind. The stillness between us.

He folds his hands behind his head, his gaze fixed on the sky. Then, he looks at me. "You're quiet."

I glance at him, smiling. "Just thinking."

"About?"

"You."

He raises an eyebrow, grinning. "What about me?"

"That you came tonight. That you're here. With me."

He reaches out, brushing a strand of hair behind my ear, fingers trailing down to the hollow of my neck.

It's so gentle I almost shiver.

"Is this okay?"

I nod, snuggling closer to him. My legs entwine with his like ivy.

His finger trembles slightly, his touch featherlight, as it

glides along the edge of my shoulder, causing the strap of my dress to slip down.

"Don't stop," I whisper.

He hesitates, his eyes searching mine like he's looking for the faintest flicker of doubt.

"Are you sure?"

I've never been this sure of anything. Not like this. And maybe tomorrow I'll overthink it.

Maybe it won't last.

But right now, I'm certain.

I grab his face, pulling him toward me, and press my lips to his. And in the silence that follows, I let myself believe, just for tonight, that this night is ours.

Chapter 28
Knight in Shining Armor
Betty

I've been staring at the crease in the yellow wallpaper for hours, my fingers absentmindedly twisting a strand of greasy hair. I sit up, grab my bag, and shrug on my cardigan. As I tiptoe down the stairs, each step creaks, loud enough to make me wince.

"Can I take the car out?" I ask, leaning over the banister.

Her voice drifts up from the dining room. "Where to?"

I step into the doorway and find Grandma sitting at the table, her Solitaire cards fanned out in perfect lines. She doesn't even look up.

"Just wanna go for a drive," I say, hugging the cardigan closer.

This time, she lifts her gaze. "Betty, you've been holed up in that room for days. What's on your mind?"

Part of me wants to tell her. About the party. About the homecoming dance. Everything. She knows how to comfort me with her gentle words and homemade chocolate chip cookies. But I know she'd telephone Mom and Dad without hesitation.

So I shake my head and say, "Nothing. I'm fine."

She studies me for a moment, then tosses me the keys. "Fill her up when you're done."

I slip out before she can change her mind.

As I turn the key in the ignition, the engine rumbles to life. It's nearly dusk, the moon is just starting to cast a pale glow over the streets as I pull out of the driveway.

The farther I drive, the fewer the houses. Just stretches of trees and radio towers blinking like Morse code. I don't know how long I've been driving or where I'm going. But I don't want to stop. I feel almost free, like if I keep going, I can pretend I'm somewhere else. Someone else. That I never kissed Miles. That James never met Cassie. That none of it ever happened.

But then, out of the corner of my eye, something moves. A flash of brown cutting across the road. I slam on the brakes, the tires screeching in protest as the car shudders violently. The car skids to a stop, but it's too late.

With trembling hands, I manage to fumble the door open and slide out of the car. My stomach twists as I take a step closer. The deer lies on the pavement, its body still as if it's only asleep.

I look around, only seeing darkness and a gas station's neon sign looming in the distance. My legs move before I can think, carrying me until I reach the payphone tucked in the corner of the parking lot. I drop a handful of coins into the slot and punch in the only number I know by heart.

The line rings twice before he picks up.

"James." My voice cracks. "I... I need you. I'm at the Marathon on Route 35. About forty miles out."

"I'm on my way," he says without hesitation.

I sit on the curb, hugging my knees as the night stretches on. The cicadas hum, the leaves rustle, and the air smells of gasoline. When I finally see the headlights of his truck, my chest loosens.

James steps out, his hair tousled like he ran his fingers through it the whole drive. "I see you're still wearing my cardigan," he says, walking toward me with a slight grin.

"I've been meaning to give it back," I say, tugging on the sleeve.

"Keep it," he says quickly. He steps closer, close enough that I can see the stubble on his jaw. "Are you okay?"

I nod, throat tightening. But then the reality hits—

"James... the car."

"We'll figure it out," he says, offering me his hand.

I hesitate before taking it. We walk back to the car together, the gravel crunching under our shoes.

James walks around the car, inspecting the damage. "Jesus," he mutters, running a hand through his hair. "My uncle knows a guy at Dawson's Auto. I'll give him a ring first thing in the morning. Let's get you home."

He opens the passenger door for me, and I slide in, the leather cold against my legs. As he starts the engine, the familiar hum of his truck fills the silence.

"James?" I say after a moment.

"Yeah?"

"Thanks for coming." I look at him, my fingers fidgeting with the sleeve of the cardigan. "I wasn't sure you'd —"

"Betty, come on," he cuts in, looking over at me. "You know I'd drop everything if you needed me." He pauses. "What were you doing out here anyway?"

"I just needed to be somewhere that wasn't my bedroom," I mumble, turning my gaze to the window.

"Do you want to talk about it?"

"I just…" I bite my lip, trying to force the lump in my throat down. "I don't know. I guess… it feels like I'm stuck in this old version of you… and I don't know where I fit anymore."

He exhales sharply, his hands curling around the steering wheel. "You're still my best friend."

"Am I?" My voice wavers slightly. "Every time I turn around, you're with her, looking at her the same way you used to look at me. It's killing me, James."

Suddenly, he veers the truck to the side of the road. He sighs, turning to face me.

"Betty," he says, almost urgently, "I don't want to lose you again. But I can't pretend like I don't care about her either. I don't know how to be who she needs and still be who I've always been with you. I'm trying to figure it out, okay?"

The weight of his words settles over me. I don't even know what I want from him anymore, but I'm pretty sure it's not this awkward, half-hearted attempt to balance everything.

I look at him, his face shadowed in the dim light of the truck.

"I'm sorry."

James exhales, the tension in his shoulders easing slightly. "You don't have to apologize," he says softly. "This is on me, too."

The truck starts moving again, but the silence between us feels heavier than before, the road ahead just as uncertain as everything between us.

Then suddenly—

"Shit." His hands tighten around the wheel, his foot pressing harder on the gas. "It's Cassie's birthday."

I blink, my stomach sinking at the mere mention of her name.

"Go to Cassie," I say, my voice steady, even if my insides feel like they're unraveling. "She's your girlfriend, after all."

And of course. It's her birthday.

Chapter 29
Any Second Now
Cassie

I check my watch. 9:12 PM.

James told me to meet him at Marg's at 8:30 PM to celebrate my birthday. But as the minutes stretch on, doubt creeps in. Nevertheless, I sit cross-legged in our regular booth, glued to the leather seat.

I glance around the diner, noticing the world moving on. Dolly, cigarette perched between her fingers, jots down orders. An old man sits alone, his newspaper wrinkled, a bowl of peach cobbler growing cold in front of him.

I check my watch again, its hands ticking slowly, each second causing my heart to crack a little more. A fly buzzes past, landing on the rim of my coffee mug. I watch the door again, willing it to swing open. Any second now.

When Dolly approaches with a pot of coffee, her eyes soften. "Do you want a pie to go?"

I shake my head, unable to tear my gaze from the door.

"We close at ten o'clock sharp," she says, blowing out a plume of smoke.

"He'll be here," I say quietly, as if to convince myself.

Fifteen minutes later, Dolly makes her way over to my booth again, carrying a slice of cherry pie adorned with a pink candle peeking out from beneath a cloud of whipped cream.

"Here you go, darling," she says, setting the plate in front of me. "Happy birthday."

I force a smile.

The clock strikes ten, and with a heavy heart, Dolly walks me to the door. "I'm sure that boy has a good explanation," she says, patting my back. "And if he doesn't..." She shakes her head. "I know a few ladies from church with bats in their trunks."

She winks and saunters away.

I glance up at the sky, searching for answers in the stars. The brief rush of a passing car provides only a momentary distraction. I begin to walk, each click of my shoes on the pavement a reminder of how the world has moved on. But I'm here, trapped in a moment that feels eternal.

From around the corner, I hear the rumble of a truck barreling around like a racehorse. Before the truck can even come to a full stop, James hops out of the truck, his face exasperated.

"Cassie, oh my god. I can explain!" He can't even catch his breath as words pour from his mouth. "I was about an hour outside of town. I was... I was helping a friend."

"A friend?" I echo, raising an eyebrow. "Who?"

He pauses, kicking a pebble with his shoe. "It was... it was Betty."

My stomach sinks.

"I — look, I didn't know I'd be gone that long, I swear. She hit a deer and was stranded."

I glare at him. "James, I've never been more embarrassed in my entire life," I snap, my voice rising. "I spent my birthday sitting alone in that diner, waiting for you to walk through those doors."

"Please, let me make it up to you," he pleads, taking my hand. "I'll buy you lunch this entire week at school."

"No." I jerk my hand away.

James steps back, his face falling.

I want to yell at him, to make him understand how hurt I am, how stupid he's made me feel. Instead, I take a deep breath, trying to steady myself, trying to hold onto the little bit of control I have left.

"I need some space, James," I say, my voice firmer this time. "Just give me some time, please."

He nods slowly, his eyes shadowed with guilt, but he doesn't argue. He knows I need this. I can see it in the way he stands there, helpless.

"Can I at least drive you home?"

I stare at him for a long moment. Part of me wants to forgive him right there. But another part, the part that counted every minute he didn't show, won't let me. I shake my head and keep walking without another word.

From behind me, I hear him say, "Happy birthday, Cassie."

I almost stop. Almost turn around.

But then, I think about that night in his truck, how close we were, how everything seemed perfect. How he held me like I mattered, like there was no one else in the world.

If that night was real, why did I spend my birthday alone?

Chapter 30
Paper Note
James

Cassie hasn't sat with me at lunch all week. She doesn't wait for me after class. In history, she bolts the second the bell rings, like she can't get away fast enough. And the worst part? I have no idea how to fix it.

I tap my foot against the floor, barely hearing Mr. Harrison drone on about the Peloponnesian War. The words blur together, meaningless. I rip a sheet of paper from my notebook and write—

Please talk to me. Just five minutes.

Folding it up, I nudge Donnie. "Pass this to Cassie."

"Sure thing," he murmurs, taking it without question.

From the corner of my eye, I catch Betty watching. Her eyes flick to mine for just a second before dropping her gaze to her notebook. I turn back to Cassie, watching as she unfolds the note. She scrunches her nose, reading it, then tucks it into her book.

Donnie leans over to me. "Hey, have you talked to Betty recently?"

I frown. "Why?"

"At the homecoming dance, she—"

"Mr. Pilgrim, no talking," Mr. Harrison interrupts.

Donnie groans loudly. "Yeah, yeah. Sorry for interrupting

your lecture on Sparta, Mr. Hair. Hey, I like that. It's ironic for someone who doesn't have any. And you know me... I love irony."

"Congratulations, Mr. Pilgrim." Mr. Harrison sighs, rubbing his temples. "Detention."

Donnie throws his hands up. "Jesus Christ, man. Again?"

The bell saves Donnie from further punishment.

Cassie bolts before I can even shove my notebook into my bag. Like she's running from me. Like she has been all week. But when I step into the hallway, she's standing there waiting.

"You wanted to talk?" she says, holding up my note.

I nod, grabbing her hand before she can change her mind. I lead her to the auditorium, where we settle into the back row. The set for *Oklahoma!* is half-finished on stage, paint cans and ladders scattered across the floor.

Cassie stares at it, unmoving. "James, I'm not mad that you missed my birthday," she begins, her voice sharp but quiet. "I'm mad that when it came down to it, you chose Betty over me. As if I were an afterthought, like I'll always come second to her."

"Tell me how to fix it." I reach for her hand. "Just tell me what you need from me."

Cassie finally looks at me. Her eyes are softer now, unsure but willing. "I need to know that I matter to you."

"You do," I say quickly, maybe too quickly. "Cassie, you do.

And I swear, from now on, I'll make sure you feel that way every single day."

Cassie nods, her fingers grazing over my hand before pulling back. "I guess we'll see." She stands, smoothing out her skirt, then walks out.

The sound of a paintbrush swiping against canvas echoes from the stage below. A stagehand coats over the old mistakes like they were never there.

For a moment, I can't stop thinking about what Donnie said back in class. What happened to Betty at the homecoming dance? And why wouldn't she tell me?

Chapter 31
Halloween
Betty

I stare out my window, watching the leaves tumble from the trees, and wonder how I survived last fall without them.

It feels like a lifetime ago that I was seeking solace in McGregor's Nook, sharing my poetry with Simon, and spending my afternoons hiding in that overstuffed chair. So much has happened since then, and I find myself wondering how different my life would be if I knew then what I know now.

Would I have been so eager to leave New York? Would I have said yes to coffee with Simon? Would I feel a little less broken?

I haven't talked to James. Not since that night. He's been wrapped up in Cassie ever since, and any chance of getting him alone feels about as likely as turning back time. It's as if everything that mattered before, everything I *thought* mattered, has just faded into the background.

Julie must've noticed it too, because she invited me to a Halloween party at Ohio University.

"You look like you could use a night out," she said to me.

At first, I wasn't sure what she meant. I wasn't even sure I'd say yes. But, after watching James and Cassie together day after day, I realized that maybe she was right.

Grandma wasn't thrilled about the idea of me going to a

college party an hour away, especially after the deer incident.

"What if you were seriously hurt or worse?!" Her voice is firm, like it always is when she's worried. "You're lucky James was able to get to you."

"I'll be careful," I say, smoothing black cat ears into my hair. "Julie's driving, and she said it's just a small get-together with her friends."

"No drinking." Her eyes narrow. "No drugs. No sex."

"Grandma," I groan, rolling my eyes. "You know I'm not like that."

I hear the honks from Julie's Volvo just as I finish drawing whiskers across my cheeks.

"I'll be home by midnight."

"Eleven o'clock.”

"Fine.” I groan louder.

When I slide into the passenger seat, Julie's already grinning at me. "Are you excited? Your first college party!"

"Thanks for inviting me," I reply with a slight smile. "I needed this."

"No problem." She glances at my cat ears, raising an eyebrow. "So, what are you supposed to be?"

"A cat." I glance at Julie, taking in her baggy Levis, red turtleneck, and glittery makeup that matches her painted nails. "What about you?"

Julie taps the steering wheel, a sly smile curling at the

corner of her mouth. "I'm changing when we get there."

I give her a skeptical look, but she's already starting the car, the engine purring to life as we pull away.

As we drive further from Gallipolis, the miles slipping by, our conversation flows from my recap of New York to Julie's decision to take a semester off from Ohio University. But then, without really meaning to, I find myself asking her what she thinks of Cassie.

"I haven't really met her," she replies, her voice steady but thoughtful. "He doesn't bring her around the house. Except — there was this one morning I caught them in the treehouse together."

My head snaps to her. "What?"

"Oh!" Her eyes widen. "I don't mean—no. Not like that."

I sigh, sinking back into my seat.

"Betty," Julie begins hesitantly. "Never mind."

"What?"

"It's nothing." She shakes her head. "Don't worry about it." She reaches over to turn the radio down. "Listen, I've been in your shoes before. I know how hard this is. But I know James. This is hard on him, too."

The autumn wind bites at my fingers as I step out of the car in front of a brick dormitory where a heavy fog hovers around it like a ghost. Julie locks her arm in mine, pulling me towards a door that's booming with music on the other side. Opening the door, my eyes scan the room.

"Hey Julie, who's the cat?" I hear a voice yell.

And then I realize — I'm the only one wearing a costume.

Julie takes my hand and pulls me into the room. "This is my friend Betty!"

The partygoers come up to introduce themselves to me. One guy with a goatee offers me a drink, but I politely decline. They're all nice, I guess. Friendly enough. Then, a guy with frosted tips suggests a game of truth or dare.

I don't know why I agree, but I do. So when it's my turn, I push my hesitation down and choose a dare.

"You sure you're up for it, Cat Girl?" the guy says, his voice too loud.

And I thought Carrot Head was bad.

"I dare you to go into the woods out back until one of us comes to get you."

I blink. "That's it?"

The group exchanges looks, the kind that make me feel like I'm missing something.

"Those woods are haunted," he says, his voice dropping. "There was an asylum on campus. Back in the '40s, one of the patients went missing. Some say the patient still wanders those woods, trying to find their way back."

I'm not going to back down. Not now. Not in front of all these strangers.

"I don't believe in ghosts." I stand up, feeling their eyes on me as I walk toward the door.

The night air is colder than I expect, the breeze sharp against my cheeks. I pull my jacket tighter, stopping for a moment to glance back at the dorm. The lights seem so far away now, like I'm already miles away.

It's too quiet.

Everything's too quiet. Every snap of a twig, every rustle of the leaves beneath my shoes makes my stomach lurch. I glance down at my mood ring, but I can't see the color. Just the shape of it, barely catching what little moonlight filters through the trees.

The minutes stretch on. Maybe it's been an hour. I don't know. I'm standing here, in the middle of the woods, wearing these stupid cat ears on my head. I yank them off and toss them to the ground.

Then I hear something. Movement behind me. I freeze.

"Hello?" My voice wobbles just a little.

Silence.

I exhale, rolling my eyes at myself. This is stupid. I don't believe in ghosts, and even if I did, the worst thing out here is probably a squirrel.

Still.

I take a cautious step back, then another. That's when I hear it... footsteps, crunching leaves. My breath catches. I turn sharply, my pulse thrumming in my ears, and then—

"Boo!" Julie stumbles into view, beer bottle in hand.

"Jesus!" My whole body deflates. "What the hell?"

She wobbles toward me. "You should've seen your face," she slurs, tapping my nose with her finger. "Classic Betty."

"You're drunk, Julie." I swat her hand away.

Julie laughs, brushing a strand of hair from her face, clearly more than a little drunk. "Calm down. It was just a game."

"Calm down?" I snap. "I've been standing out here for god knows how long. And you... you didn't tell me nobody else was going to wear a costume!"

Julie blinks at me like she's trying to process my words through a fog. "I thought you knew." Her face falls. "I wasn't trying to embarrass you. I'm sorry."

I cross my arms, annoyed.

"Look, I'm sorry we left you out here so long." She blinks, like she's fighting to stay focused. "We lost track of time and—" Her voice trails off, and she drops her head in shame.

"Can we just go?"

Julie sways a little, looking down at the bottle in her hand. "You'll have to drive."

I sigh, but I don't say anything. Looping my arm under hers, we make our way back to the car. I slide into the driver's seat, gripping the steering wheel. Glancing back at the woods, I swear I see something move. Maybe it's nothing. Or maybe the woods aren't haunted.

Maybe I am.

Chapter 32
Dinner and a Show

James

We haven't hosted Thanksgiving since Mom died. Cassie should be here any minute, and I want everything to go smoothly.

"Hey, James, where's the mashed potatoes?" Julie calls from the dining room.

"Coming right up!"

Just as I set the dish on the counter, the doorbell rings. I wipe my hands on a dish towel and head to the door. Swinging it open, I'm greeted by Betty, holding a pumpkin pie. Behind her is her grandma, Dorothea, who looks as cheerful as ever.

"What are you doing here?" I blurt out.

"Oh, your darling father invited us!" Dorothea replies, stepping inside as if she owns the place. "He felt bad that Betty wouldn't be spending Thanksgiving with her parents."

"I hope that's okay?" Betty adds.

"I'm just a little surprised, that's all," I say, ushering them inside.

Julie appears from the dining room, her eyes wide as she registers the scene. "What a surprise!" She opens her arms and pulls Betty in for a hug.

"Dad!" I stride into the kitchen where he's slicing away at the turkey. "Why did you invite Betty without telling me first?"

"I didn't think it would be an issue," he mutters, barely looking up from the poor, unfortunate bird he's attacking.

The doorbell rings.

I head back to the living room, the tension coiling inside me like a spring. My fingers tremble as I reach for the door knob, and with a deep breath, I open it. Cassie walks in, her smile bright but faltering as she glances past me at Betty.

"Happy Thanksgiving, Cassie," I say, my voice catching slightly. "This is my sister, Julie."

Julie ambles over, extending her hand. "I've heard so much about you."

Dad appears from the kitchen, his hands covered in turkey juices. "You must be Cassie! Well, now that everyone's here, let's get settled at the table."

Julie puts her hand up, stepping toward Dad. "Not everyone *is* here. I invited a friend. His name is Rusty."

I shoot a glare at Julie. "Who's Rusty?"

She smirks. "Just a friend I know from school."

"Well, the more the merrier," Dorothea chirps, clapping her hands together.

I brace myself as the doorbell rings again. In walks a guy with long black hair cascading down to his shoulders. He's wearing a Nirvana shirt, baggy jeans, and black Doc Martens. A tattoo of a tree stretches across his forearm, its intricate branches reaching out as he moves. There's a faint smell trailing behind him — skunk, maybe?

Dad marches toward the door, hands on his hips. "I assume you're Rusty?"

"Yes, sir," Rusty says, extending his hand. "It's a pleasure to meet you, Mr. Cohen."

"It's Sheriff Cohen to you." Dad glares at him for a moment, then steps back, eyes still narrowed. "Alright, then. Let's get settled at the table."

We all shuffle into the dining room. I take my seat, glancing at Betty, who's directly across from me. Cassie shifts in her seat beside me, clearly uncomfortable. I take a deep breath, trying to shake off the unease bubbling up inside of me, but it lingers like the scent of burnt turkey.

Julie, on the other hand, seems to be enjoying the scene entirely too much. Rusty plops down next to her, and as he does, he leans back in his chair, making it creak ominously.

"So Rusty," Dad begins. "What are you studying in school?"

Rusty looks up, slightly confused. "Oh, I'm not in school."

"That's funny," Dad begins, dishing himself cranberry sauce. "Julie mentioned that she knew you from school."

"High school, Dad," Julie clarifies.

Dad narrows his eyes. "So you're not in college?"

"No, sir, I work for my pop's pool cleaning business."

"Pool cleaning business?" Dad crosses his arms. "We live in Ohio. Business can't be *that* good."

"Hey, I can't complain." Rusty shrugs, still grinning. "I like being outside, working with my hands. And I'm learning a lot about running a business."

"And what do you do the other nine months of the year?" Dad leans forward, glaring at Rusty. "Smoke the devil's lettuce and play video games?"

"Dad!" Julie snaps, rolling her eyes.

"College isn't for everyone," I add, trying to support Julie. "Look at Bill Gates. He dropped out of Harvard, and he's doing fine."

"At least Rusty knows what he wants," Betty smirks. "And what do you want, James?" She pauses, clearly suppressing a laugh. "To pass geometry? You barely passed without copying my homework."

"Actually," Cassie pipes up. "I've been tutoring him."

"Yeah?" Betty raises an eyebrow. "And how is that working out for you, James?"

"Well, I managed to get a B on my last quiz," I say, trying to keep it casual.

"That's great, James!" Dorothea says from the end of the table. "When I worked at the high school, your mother always told her students that learning takes time. It's about progress, not perfection."

"Exactly." Rusty nods thoughtfully. "I didn't ace high school, but look at me now!"

"Look at you indeed," Dad says, taking a bite of turkey.

"Let's change the subject, please," Julie scolds, shooting Dad a glare.

"James," Dorothea begins, folding her hands like she's settling in for a story. "Why don't you tell us how you met Cassie?"

I watch as Betty shrinks into her chair, stuffing her face with mashed potatoes.

"I met her last December," I begin, watching Betty out of the corner of my eye. "We were working at the soup kitchen together."

"I called him a few weeks later," Cassie adds with a smile. "We ended up talking for hours."

Betty finally looks up. "Hours? Must've really lost track of time." She pauses just long enough to let the silence stretch, then mutters, "Is that all you lost?"

Julie snorts into her water glass.

My cheeks flush, and before I can stop myself, I kick Betty under the table.

"James, why don't you and Betty grab the pies in the kitchen?" Dad says, rubbing his hands together with anticipation. "I'm ready for dessert."

I glance at Betty, who looks just as unenthused.

As we walk to the kitchen, my heart races. I quickly step forward, cornering her against the refrigerator. "What the hell,

Betty!" I snap, lowering my voice. "Are you trying to make this dinner worse than it already is?"

"And what?" she scoffs. "You think I'm having the time of my life here — sitting across the table from your girlfriend while your dad interrogates the stoner?"

She pushes off from the refrigerator, stepping closer. I suddenly become aware of how close we are, so close that I can smell her vanilla perfume. My pulse quickens even more.

"Then why did you come?"

Betty hesitates, her playful demeanor fading. "I don't know, James. Maybe I didn't want to spend my Thanksgiving watching the Macy's parade with my grandma."

I look away, jaw tightening. "You're exhausting, you know that?"

"Don't pretend you don't love it."

I almost smile. Almost.

"Let's just... get through tonight, okay?" I say, a reluctant smile breaking through. "But if you keep making snarky comments, I'll kick you out of the house."

"Fair enough." A smirk tugs at the corner of her lips. "Though I think your dad might toss Rusty out first."

I chuckle, grabbing the pumpkin pie.

As we return to the dining room, I notice Cassie glancing between us, her expression curious, though she doesn't say anything.

Later that night, after all the food was eaten and the dishes were wiped clean, I said goodbye to Cassie, then to Rusty, and finally to Dorothea and Betty. But even after Betty's gone, I can still feel the weight of her presence, like she never really left.

Chapter 33
Clara
Cassie

I'm backstage, trying to steady my breath as I hear the muffled sounds of the audience settling into their seats. I've rehearsed for months. Bled through pointe shoes. Practiced lifts with a partner who kept dropping me.

I'm playing Clara tonight, the role every ballerina dreams of playing. I should feel exhilarated. Tonight is supposed to be my night.

I hear the pianist strike a chord, and suddenly, I'm being ushered onto the stage. The moment I step out under the spotlight, I search the darkened theater, hoping to spot my parents in the crowd. A part of me is convinced they'll be here. Maybe, just this once, they'll show up. But I don't see them.

The stage lights are hot, blinding almost. I take a deep breath, my body moving through the routine. My heart is pounding in my chest, my palms slick with sweat. I glance at the other dancers around me, their faces focused, bright with enthusiasm, and I push the sadness down, forcing a smile.

The final curtain draws thunderous applause, but it isn't enough to erase the emptiness I feel. I rush backstage, still catching my breath as I step into the dressing room. The other girls chatter amongst themselves as they unlace their pointe shoes, peeling off layers of tulle.

"My mom brought the biggest bouquet! I swear it's bigger than my head."

"I can't believe my dad actually cried watching me dance. He never cries."

I sit down at my vanity, my fingers quivering as I reach up to take out my hairpins. I glance at my reflection, cheeks still flushed, mascara smudged at the corners of my eyes.

I pull my coat tight around myself, feeling smaller than I should as I leave the auditorium. I wait by the stage door for a few minutes, pretending I'm checking my hair, hoping maybe I just missed them. It's a little after ten. Maybe they'll still make it. But no one is coming.

With a heavy sigh, I pick up my bag and turn to leave. The cold air bites at my skin the second I push through the door. The parking lot is nearly empty now. Just a few scattered cars and the dull glow of the street lights reflecting off patches of ice on the pavement.

I round the corner of the building, my head bowed against the cold wind. And then — footsteps. My heart jumps before I even see him. His jacket is slightly askew like he's been in a hurry, and his hair's all tousled, like he's been dragging his hands through it nonstop. He doesn't even look like himself.

He looks like a kid who got caught sneaking out.

"James," I say, a little too quickly, trying to keep my tone steady. "What are you doing here?"

"I-I was just... leaving work. Al kept me late. You know how he is." He lets out an awkward laugh, rubbing the back of his neck. Then, he takes a step toward me, his face filled with that same apologetic look he always wears when he feels like he's disappointed someone.

"I was hoping to make it to your show in time, Cass. I'm sorry. I just..." He trails off, pushing his boots into the snow.

"It's okay," I say, but it's too sharp. I sound more defensive than I want to, like I'm trying to convince myself more than him. Then, before I can stop myself, I blurt, "You were coming from Maple?"

James' eyebrows shoot up in surprise.

"You were walking from Maple Avenue, right?" I say, a little more firmly now. "Al's Market is on the other side of town."

I know what's on Maple Avenue. How could I forget?

"Right," James says, looking over his shoulder at the street sign. "Yeah, I guess I was. I mean, I didn't have a destination in mind. I was just... walking. Long day at work." His eyes drop, like he's thinking about something... or someone else entirely.

I could push him. I could ask why he was really over there. But if I ask, I might not like the answer. So I just nod and pretend it doesn't matter.

"Cass, I..." He trails off. "I should go."

He quickly bends down and places a kiss on my cheek. And

then, without another word, he turns and walks away.

I stand there for a moment, watching him leave, feeling the chill of the air sink deeper into my bones. I want to believe that he came all this way for me — that he ran from Al's Market hoping to catch the last few minutes of the show. Maybe he was planning to surprise me with flowers.

But he didn't. And I think that's what hurts the most.

Chapter 34
The Turret
Betty

Grandma's snow boots thump against the hardwood, pulling me out of my thoughts. I glance up just as she steps into the room, a small box in her hands, and a grin stretches across her face.

"The postman just dropped this off. It's for you, dear!"

I pick it up, turning the box over in my hands. The return address reads New York City. Mom's handwriting is scrawled across the label.

"It's from my parents."

"Oh, perhaps it's an early Christmas gift," Grandma muses.

I tear into the package, expecting a sweater or maybe a book, but when I peel back the tissue paper, I freeze. Nestled inside is a plastic brick with a tiny screen and rubber buttons.

Grandma leans over for a better look. "What in the Lord's name is that?"

I stare at the clunky device in my palm. "It's a phone." I frown, flipping it over.

She watches me for a moment, then gently pats my knee. "Mind doing me a favor?"

I glance up, more grateful than I want to admit for something to do.

"I'm hosting my annual cookie exchange tonight," she says,

already rising from her chair. "Think you could pop over to the market and grab a few things?"

As I mosey down the aisles of Al's Market, the scent of bread fills the air, mixing with the sound of Dean Martin singing some holiday song about snow. I turn the corner to grab some flour, and then I freeze. There's James, stocking the shelves with cans of Campbell's soup.

"James?"

He looks up, a sheepish grin spreading across his face. Something flutters in my stomach — quiet, unexpected, and impossible to ignore.

"Is this how you're going to be spending your winter break?" I chuckle, picking up a can of soup. "Stocking shelves at Al's Market?"

"Well, I get Christmas Day off." He shrugs. "What are you doing here?"

"Oh, I've been tasked with gathering some ingredients for my grandma's cookie exchange tonight," I say, shoving my hands into my coat pockets.

"Ah, yes," James says with a smile. "The town's most coveted invite of the year. My mom used to go to those every year before—" His voice trails off momentarily. Then he clears his throat.

Without thinking, I blurt, "Wanna come?"

His face lights up in a way that I haven't seen in a long

time. He suddenly bumps the shelf, sending a can of soup tumbling to the floor with a loud clang, loud enough to make three people turn and stare.

He laughs. "I get off at 8."

Later that night, the guests begin trickling in one by one into the warmth of the Victorian house. But not us.

We race across the yard, our boots crunching against the thick blanket of snow. I scoop up a handful of snow, packing it tightly and hurling it at James. Then we collapse, breathless.

"Do you remember that blizzard a few years ago?" James asks, his lips fading to purple. "We made that huge blanket fort in the living room. And we had to defend our fortress from the invading forces—"

"Julie," we say in unison.

"You were the ultimate commander," he reminisces. "And I was your loyal soldier."

As the icy wind picks up, I shiver, wrapping my arms around myself. "Okay, I'm freezing," I say, my teeth chattering slightly.

"Yeah, me too," James replies, his frozen plume floating in the air.

As we retreat inside, James opens the creaky wooden cupboard and pulls out a bottle of whiskey, his eyes mischievous.

"How about we add a little warmth to this night?"

We settle into the turret, stealing a plate of Mrs. Pilgrim's snickerdoodle cookies.

Every time I sit in the turret of the Victorian house, I pretend I'm a princess in a fairy tale — trapped, waiting for my knight in shining armor to climb the tower and rescue me. But tonight, sitting in the dimly lit turret with James, I don't feel trapped. I feel hopeful.

I take a swig of whiskey, immediately grimacing as it scorches down my throat. "Oh god... that's awful!" I wince, wiping my mouth with the back of my hand.

James laughs, snatching the bottle back. "Can't be as bad as that time I dared you to drink the creek water. I thought for sure you'd be puking all summer."

I laugh, shaking my head. "You were such a menace."

"Hey, not my fault you never backed down from a dare," he chuckles, nudging my knee.

A quiet settles between us. Not awkward — just familiar.

"Do you remember when we used to catch tadpoles?" The words come softly, like they've been waiting months to be said. "Everything was so simple back then."

"I remember," he says, smiling. "And when you worked up the courage to swing across the creek."

"I screamed the whole way."

He laughs. "That might've been the moment I fell in love with you."

I look at him. "James, we were seven."

He shrugs, eyes locked on mine.

The candle flickers, casting our shadows on the wall. I stare out at the falling snow through the stained glass window.

James digs in his jacket pocket, pulling out a cassette case.

"Here," he says. "This is for you."

I blink.

"It's the tape," he adds quickly. "The one I made for your birthday." He places it on the floor between us.

"Man," I say, picking it up and turning it over in my hand. "Never thought I'd get a James Cohen mixtape ever again."

I run a thumb over the label. In his messy handwriting, it says *For Betty* — nothing more. Nothing less.

Just those two words.

I want to tell him how moments like this make me feel — how I could stay here forever in this turret, just the two of us. I wonder if he feels it too, the way the air shifts when we're this close.

"Betty," he whispers.

Suddenly, his hands reach for my cheeks, slowly pulling me toward him. And then his lips press against mine. It feels so easy, so achingly familiar. The kiss deepens, and his hand slides to the back of my neck, fingers threading through my hair.

But then — it's like a light switch flicks on.

I see Cassie, her hands holding my hair back. The memory jolts me, and I pull back slightly, my breath hitching as the weight of what we're doing settles in my chest.

"James," I manage to say, pulling away. "We can't do this."

For a moment, we sit in silence, both caught in the weight of what just happened.

He stands, shoving his hands into his pockets. "I should go."

As he reaches the door, he pauses, glancing back at me one last time. He looks hurt. The same confused expression James wore that day when I asked if he loved Cassie. Only this time, I think he knows the answer.

The door clicks shut behind him.

I sit there, hugging my knees and staring at the closed door, feeling this hollow ache. For a moment, I want to run after him, to tell him to come back. But I stay put, reminding myself that sometimes the right thing feels all wrong.

Chapter 35
The Letter
James

I wake up later than usual. No early shift at Al's, no alarm beeping in my ear — just the soft light of a Saturday morning. Then I see the envelope on my desk waiting for me. My hands are shaking before I even pick it up.

Dear Mr. Cohen,

I am writing to inform you that the Committee on Admissions cannot, at this time, make a final decision on your application for a place in next year's entering class. However, the Committee has voted to place your name on a wait-list for whom we hope places may become available later.

I fall back on my bed with a loud groan.

Julie knocks on my door. "What's up? I heard that groan from my room."

"Waitlisted." I hold up the letter. "Maybe I'm fooling myself," I grumble. "I'm just a guy from Ohio with average grades and a part-time job at a grocery store. NYU was a long shot."

"A lot of successful people were born in Ohio," she says, plopping down on my bed. "And besides, being waitlisted isn't a rejection." She searches my eyes. "Is there something else going on? You've seemed distracted lately."

I open my mouth. Close it. Then groan, dragging my hands down my face. "I kissed Betty."

She looks at me with a slight smirk. "I thought we made a deal that you were going to figure out your love life... not make it worse."

I peek through my fingers. "Yeah? What about *your* love life? Whatever happened to that Rusty guy you invited to Thanksgiving?"

"Oh, *him*," she chuckles. "James, we were never an item."

I blink, confused. "But, Thanksgiving?"

"He was more so... an ice breaker," she says slowly. "I knew that things would be awkward with Betty and Cassie *both* being at the dinner table." She shrugs. "So I invited an old friend to lighten the mood. And I invited the one guy I knew would get under Dad's skin. It made for a very entertaining meal."

"Wait-wait-wait," I stammer. "You *knew* that Dad invited Betty... and you didn't warn me?!"

"Now, where's the fun in that? It was hilarious watching you squirm."

I groan, leaning back in my chair. "You've got a twisted sense of humor, you know that?"

Julie's smirk fades, her body stiffening. "James, there's something I need to tell you," she begins, her voice low. "Just, promise you won't get mad."

My eyes narrow. "Okay?"

She hesitates. "I-I found Betty's letter."

My stomach drops.

"It must have gotten lost in the mail. And when I found it, you were already with Cassie."

I shake my head in frustration. "Why would you keep something like this from me?"

"I didn't want to complicate things!" she snaps. "You were finally happy again after —"

"Would you stop meddling with my life?" I interject, my voice cracking. "I'm not a kid anymore!"

"I know, and I'm sorry. I really am."

The room goes quiet.

Finally, I exhale. "Can I at least read it?"

She exits my room, returning with a small envelope in her hand. "I almost told her. On Halloween."

I look at her. "Why didn't you?"

"I don't know." She pauses. "I started to. But I couldn't."

Julie lingers for a second, like she wants to say more, then she just nods and turns toward the door. Her footsteps are quiet, and the door clicks shut behind her.

My fingers tremble as I unfold the letter, the paper wrinkled like it's been held too tightly, too many times. The ink is smudged in places, and then I notice dried water droplets dotting the page.

"Dear James,

I need to tell you the truth.

I haven't made any friends. Not one. I try to pretend I'm okay, but the truth is, I'm not. I read your letters so many times, I've memorized every word. I wish I could go back to that summer day we carved our names into the tree and stay there forever.

Yours always,
Betty"

I remember that summer day. The way the bark flaked beneath my pocketknife's blade. The sunburn peeling on her shoulders. We carved our names into the walnut tree like it meant something permanent, like the creek belonged to us and always would.

I squeeze my eyes shut, sinking to the floor, but it doesn't stop the guilt from clawing its way through my chest. She waited. Months. Checked the mailbox every day, hoping for a letter that never came. And the worst part?

She never stopped hoping. Not even after I did.

Chapter 36
Goose

Betty

It's been a month since I last spoke to James. Since the cookie exchange. Since the kiss.

I've been diving into the stack of novels Grandma got me for Christmas. They're a welcome distraction, but I can't bring myself to retreat to the turret to read or write like I used to. It feels like that space has been tainted.

Instead, I find solace on the front porch swing. Even in the midst of January's biting cold, there's something comforting about wrapping myself in a floral quilt and losing myself in a book.

Grandma joins me on the porch, her knitting needles clicking softly as she settles into her favorite wicker chair. We engage in light conversation, discussing everything from the weather to the latest gossip in town.

And then she asks me, "Have you thought about what colleges you want to apply to yet?"

To be honest, I haven't given it much thought since I got home, so I just shrug. It's hard to picture the future when the present still feels so blurry. I glance down at my book, tracing the edge of the crimson lapel pin that Mr. McGregor gave me.

"Betty," Grandma begins gently, "I want you to know that no matter where you go, you will always have a home here."

"I know." I look at her, a slight smile tugging on my lips. "Gallipolis will always be my home."

"That's not what I mean," Grandma says, looping her yarn through her needles."You'll always have a place to come back to. Here. On Maple Avenue." Her eyes dart up to meet mine. "I've made sure of it."

"This house?"

She looks at me with a slight grin and then winks.

"I-I don't know what to say."

She lifts a hand. "Then don't. Not until I'm dead."

I lean back in my seat, letting the quilt hug my shoulders as I imagine myself sitting on this same porch fifty years from now. I smile at the thought, at the quiet, the comfort. But then another thought creeps in, quieter still.

Who will be sitting beside me?

Suddenly, I hear a car door slam shut. Footsteps. Luggage wheels scraping against the pavement. I blink, sitting upright. And then I see her standing on the sidewalk, suitcase in hand.

"Mom?" I blink. "What are you doing here? I thought you and Dad weren't coming back until graduation."

"Change of plans," she says, opening her arms for a hug.

I throw my book down and run into her arms.

"Did you get our Christmas gift? The cell phone?" she asks, pulling back just enough to look at me.

"Yeah, I got it," I say.

She laughs, brushing a strand of hair from my face. "Your dad insisted. But I knew you'd hate it."

I snort. "I didn't hate it. I just... don't see the point of having it."

She grins. "He said, 'Mark my words, in a few years, everyone is going to have one of those things strapped to their hip.'"

I roll my eyes.

Grandma looks at us with a grin. "Why don't you two head inside to warm up? I'm sure you have lots to catch up on."

Mom smiles, already pulling me toward the stairs. "Come on, we can talk while you help me unpack."

The floor creaks under our weight as we settle on the bed. She unzips her suitcase and begins folding sweaters and trousers, stacking them in the drawers.

She pauses, glancing over her shoulder. "So," she says lightly, "what's going on between you and James?"

"What do you mean?" I try to play it off, but I can feel my cheeks burning.

She raises an eyebrow. "I heard that he came to the cookie exchange, and you two snuck off together."

"He kissed me." I glance down, twisting the thread on my sleeve. "In the turret."

For a moment, I can still feel his cold hands on my cheeks.

The taste of whiskey on his lips.

"I kissed him back," I admit. "I wanted to. But it didn't feel right." I stare at my hands. "Now everything is confusing."

She exhales, resting a hand on the folded clothes in her lap. "Love can be like that." Something in her tone softens. She hesitates, smoothing the edge of a sweater. "Goose, there's something I've been meaning to tell you."

I shift uncomfortably. "What is it?"

She sighs. "Your dad and I... we're getting a divorce."

It's as though the floor crumbled beneath me.

"I-I don't understand," I manage. "When I left New York, everything was fine."

"We haven't been fine for a long time," she says gently. "New York just made it clearer."

I sit in silence, stunned. "Did I do something wrong?"

"Oh, Goose, no." She brushes a hair behind my ear. "Things change. People change. That's just life." She takes a breath. "Did I ever tell you how we met?"

"At a club in Athens," I say, still dazed.

"The Gilded Goose." She nods with a smile. "That's where I got your nickname."

She meets my eye, then continues. "I had just finished singing with my band, The Nightingales." She smiles faintly, the memory lighting something behind her eyes. "He walked up to me and told me I sang like Joni Mitchell. Then asked if I wanted to get pancakes." She chuckles to herself. "It was nearly midnight, but I said yes." Her eyes go distant. "Three months later, I was pregnant with you."

I swallow hard.

"We got married in the backyard here," she reminisces. "The wedding was small and perfect in every way. And we were happy — for a while." She reaches out to grasp my hand. "Goose, I want you to know that you are the daughter of two people who love you very much. That will never change."

"How did you know?" I begin softly. "How did you know that it was time to let go of each other?"

Her eyes search mine. "Is this about James?"

My throat tightens, and I glance away.

"Goose, my situation with your father is worlds apart from yours with James." She pauses. "We barely had time to get acquainted before diving into marriage and parenthood. But you've known James your whole life, way before romance even entered the equation."

I feel tears welling in my eyes, and I lay my head in her lap.

She combs her fingers through my hair. "Your bond with James is so special. I know it hurts now, but soulmates have a way of finding their way back to each other. Maybe not right away. Maybe not even in the way you expect. But love like that doesn't just vanish."

She squeezes my hand. "And even if it does... that just

makes room for something new. Something unexpected. Something that's still beautiful. Maybe it's time you find out who Betty Thompson is — *without* James. Just you."

I stay curled in her lap even after her words fade into silence. And slowly, it hits me just how much I missed this. The comfort of her arms, the soft hum of her breath, the faint scent of lavender clinging to her sweater.

Like home, like before.

Chapter 37
Splinters
Cassie

I pick at my dinner, overcooked steak and instant mashed potatoes. My parents sit across from me in the cramped dining room of our house. The table is old, its wood chipped and peeling, years of wear splintering at the edges. I trace my fingers over a rough patch, feeling the tiny ridges bite into my skin.

Splinters. That's what this house is. That's what we are. Little broken pieces of something that used to be whole.

I glance at them, and with a steady breath, I say, "I think I want to take a gap year next year. After graduation."

Dad scoffs, dropping his fork onto his plate. "A gap year? And do what?"

"I don't know," I say, gripping my jeans under the table. "I just... I feel like I need some time to find myself."

"Find yourself?" Mom laughs, setting her wine glass down. "Is this because you realized no school's going to take you seriously? Not after what happened in Cincinnati."

"You don't even know the full story." My grip on my jeans tightens. "You don't want to hear it."

"I don't want to hear your excuses." Her face tightens. "We're already wasting enough money on those silly ballet classes."

She used to braid my hair before every recital. Now, she can't even look at me when I speak. Mom takes another sip of her wine and doesn't say anything else.

"At least I'm working to better myself." My fists clench at my sides. "Did you even know I have a boyfriend? That I made the Honor Roll last semester? Or that I played the role of Clara in the Nutcracker?" I hesitate, feeling my eyes brimming with tears. I swipe at my eyes and add, "You don't know me anymore."

I don't wait for them to respond. I leave, slipping out the front door and into the cold night. The stars are dull tonight, smothered by the gray clouds rolling in. I find myself walking toward the dance studio without even thinking.

I flip on the light and pull my hair into a bun. I start with a plié. Then another. My body protests, but I keep going.

Jetés. Pirouettes. Faster. Sharper.

I immerse myself in the music playing only in my head, dancing until my breath comes in ragged gasps. Each movement is a scream I was too weak to let out. Each landing, a splinter cracking further down the grain.

My foot slips during a turn, and I stumble to the floor, catching myself on my hands. I curl in on myself, fists pressed to my eyes as the sobs break through.

They will never see me the way they used to. Maybe that's okay. Because I'm not her anymore.

Chapter 38
Kanawha
Betty

The beginning of spring always marked two things: Twisty's Ice Cream Shop opening for the season and the upperclassmen camping trip at Kanawha State Forest. A nice refresh after an endless February full of gloomy overcast days and brown slush clinging to the curbs.

Shortest month of the year, yet it felt eternal.

As the bus bumps along the road, I catch glimpses of Cassie and James curled up together in their seats. Her head rests on his shoulder, and his hand is loosely tangled in hers. I turn away, focusing instead on the peeling vinyl seat in front of me.

I'm wedged between the window and Donnie, who's snoring louder than a chainsaw, his mouth slightly open.

And then I hear a laugh, the same one I heard that night at Nina's party. I grip the seat in front of me and force myself to breathe. Miles is on this bus. Only a few rows back. I can feel it. Like heat radiating off a stove.

Donnie shifts beside me. He blinks and glances my way.

"You okay?"

"Just tired."

He cracks the bus window. "If you have to throw up, aim that way."

Across the aisle, James turns his head, our eyes meeting

briefly. Then Cassie stirs against him, and he looks down at her. Of course he does. I'm not the center of his universe anymore.

I stare out the window and count the trees as they blur past. By the time I reach one hundred and eighty-nine, the bus jerks to a stop, and the trees are replaced by the gravel parking lot.

I hoist my Care Bear suitcase onto my shoulder and follow the crowd toward the cabins. Birds screech overhead like they're laughing at us. A breeze stirs the branches above, sending a soft rain of pine needles to the gravel.

The cabins sit ahead, hunched in the clearing like they don't really want us here. One of them sags slightly to the left, its wooden siding warped and coated in moss.

I trail behind the others, my suitcase bumping against my leg with every step. Every crunch of gravel feels too loud. Like the trees are listening. But beneath it all, there's this stillness — a quiet that seeps into my bones and makes me feel like if I shouted, the forest wouldn't hear me.

The inside of the cabin smells like mildew. I pick the top bunk closest to the window, not because I want the view, but because I want an exit.

I glance down and see a dead fly on the windowsill — legs curled inward, wings bent at odd angles like the poor thing gave up mid-flight. There's something sad about it. Like maybe it got stuck, buzzing for help until it just stopped.

A voice from below startles me from my thoughts.

"Is this bunk taken?"

I peer my head over and see Cassie, holding her duffel bag that's about as big as her body.

Is she serious right now? Of all the bunks in all the cabins in all of West Virginia, she picks mine.

For a second, I wonder if she's doing this on purpose... just to get under my skin. And then I remember — I'm not the center of her universe either.

I force a smile. "Sure."

I roll onto my side, pressing my face into my pillow like it might smother the urge to scream. But here, in the middle of the woods, there's no point.

Chapter 39
The Jester
James

I lay in my bunk, burying myself in a book. But then, I hear a snickering that makes my skin crawl. Glancing up, I see Donnie sitting alone by the back window, his shoulders hunched, eyes locked on the floor. Miles looms over him like a vulture circling its prey.

My eyes scan the cabin. No one else seems to notice or care. My chest tightens with frustration.

"Come on, man, leave him alone," I finally say.

Miles's head snaps toward me. He straightens up, abandoning Donnie, and makes his way over to my bunk.

"What's up with you, man?"

I don't look up. "What do you mean?"

"Besides the fact that you're defending that queer?"

A few guys chuckle, whispering to each other, clearly entertained by the spectacle.

"This whole year, you've been avoiding me," he adds. "You don't even look at me during student council meetings."

"I have a lot going on," I mumble, still refusing to meet his eyes.

Miles snorts. "What's going on with you and Betty?"

"I don't know." I slam the book shut. "Things are complicated."

"Complicated?" Miles raises an eyebrow, his smirk growing. "What, did you kiss her or something?"

My jaw tightens.

"Oh shit." He takes a step back. "You did... didn't you?"

I grit my teeth, fighting the urge to snap. "What are you getting at?"

"Well, I was just thinking about asking her to prom."

I'm on my feet before I even realize it, fists clenching at my sides. "Don't even think about it."

Miles smirks, but it falters just a little. "Relax, man. It was a joke."

"No, it wasn't." I shake my head. "Not to you. Not with her."

"What is this, some kind of white knight act?" He lets out a low, bitter laugh.

I don't answer.

"Come on, Cohen — she was the one who came on to me. *She* kissed me."

"You need to shut your mouth," I growl, stepping forward.

He tilts his head. "Why?"

I feel it in my gut before I even speak. That low, sour coil of fear. But I speak anyway.

"You assaulted her!" I roar, shoving him.

He slams into the bunk, the wood creaking under the force. For a moment, everyone in the cabin goes quiet.

"Well, I'll be damned," Miles chuckles, stepping toward me. "Our little James Cohen finally grew a pair."

Then he swings.

His fist collides with my mouth. I stumble back, my hand flying to my lip, where blood begins to trickle down my chin. I barely have time to think before the second punch comes — straight to the eye. Everything spins. I stagger back, slamming into the cabin wall behind me.

The door bursts open. Mr. Harrison storms in, followed by Donnie, who's pale and wide-eyed.

"What the hell is going on here?" Mr. Harrison barks. "You two," he points at us, "pack your bags. You're going home."

With my hand pressed against my throbbing eye, I can't help but wonder what the hell I was thinking — starting a fight with Miles, an athlete with more muscle strength than I'll ever have. Not my brightest idea.

But for Betty, it was worth it.

Chapter 40
The Girls We Could Have Been
Cassie

I lay in my bunk quietly, cocooning myself with the itchy blankets and trying not to make a sound. Maybe I'm a fool for picking the bunk directly under Betty, but I didn't have a choice. All the other bunks were taken.

Eventually, the chatter in the cabin fades to whispers as the girls begin to fall asleep one by one. Just as I close my eyes, I hear a quiet creak from above — a shift in the mattress.

"Cassie? Are you awake?"

I almost pretend to be asleep. But I don't. Because something in her voice tells me this is important. I peer my head out from the bunk and see Betty looking down at me.

"I am now," I whisper.

"Can we talk?"

After a silent nod, I watch her descend from her bunk and join me.

"Cassie I—" She pauses. "I never thanked you... for saving me that night. Instead, I've been so unkind since the day I met you." She sighs. "I think I convinced myself to hate you because it was easier than admitting how much I envied you."

"Betty, I want you to know that I never intended to come between you and James. I don't know the whole story, but I respect your feelings... and your history with him."

"God, I can see why he likes you so much," she says quietly. "You're a good person, Cassie. A genuinely good person."

There's a moment of pause, interrupted only by the snoring of one of the other girls.

"But, I'm not," I whisper.

"What do you mean?"

"At my old school," I begin, tentatively. "I was so desperate to fit in that I started hanging out with the wrong crowd." I pause, swallowing the lump rising in my throat. "There was this one girl, and we... we bullied her. Relentlessly. She didn't deserve it. No one does."

I blink, trying to hold back the tears threatening to spill. "Her parents got involved, and the school couldn't ignore it anymore. The other girls turned on me. And just like that, I was the scapegoat." My breath hitches. "I got expelled."

Betty looks down, her fingers brushing a wrinkle in the blanket. She doesn't say anything. Just listens.

"After that, everything fell apart." I pause, the words stuck in my throat. "My parents were humiliated. Moving here was supposed to be a clean slate — a chance to start over."

I can feel Betty's eyes on me, and for a moment, I brace myself for the judgment I'm sure is coming.

"I've been trying to make things right — to be a better person," I say quietly. "But I know that no matter what I do, I can never undo the pain I caused."

Betty finally speaks, her voice careful, but not unkind. "People mess up, Cassie. We all do. It's part of growing up." She pauses, her gaze thoughtful. "I think the fact that you're trying to change means something." She offers a small, tentative smile. "At least, it does to me."

I blink back tears. "I couldn't tell James. About any of this. I couldn't risk losing the only person who saw the good in me."

"I know what it's like," she says softly, "to feel alone and ashamed. But I've been learning to forgive myself."

I let out a shaky breath, the tension easing from my shoulders. "Thank you," I say. "For understanding."

Eventually, we bid each other goodnight, settling into our bunks with a newfound sense of peace. As I drift off, I wonder if the girl I used to be would even recognize the one I am now.

Maybe it's not too late. Maybe I still have a chance — not just at friendship, but at forgiveness. But even then, some part of me still wonders if I deserve it.

Chapter 41
Cherry Lollipop
Betty

I stand at my locker, shuffling through the clutter of books and second-semester papers. Just as I'm about to close my locker, Donnie appears beside me, his cheeks tinged red. I sigh inwardly, bracing myself.

"Betty," he starts, his tone unsteady. "Can I ask you something?"

My stomach tightens. I know what's coming.

"I was wondering..." He pauses, then blurts, "Look, I practiced this whole John Cusack-style speech in the mirror, and then I forgot all of it, so — will you go to prom? With me?"

I knew it.

"Donnie, I—"

Before I can finish, James and Cassie walk past hand in hand. I watch them the whole way, unable to tear my gaze away. James doesn't look my way. Not once.

Donnie steps closer, leaning in slightly. "It sucks, doesn't it? Pretending it doesn't bother you."

I frown. "What do you mean?"

He hesitates, then leans forward slightly. "Do you remember Mrs. Griffin's 6th-grade class? Valentine's Day?"

I nod, unsure where he's going with this.

"You remember how we had to hand out Valentines to

everyone in class?" He shifts uncomfortably. "James handed out his store-bought Star Wars ones like it was nothing."

"What's your point?" I reply, raising an eyebrow.

"Yours was different," he continues. "Your Valentine was handmade and had a cherry lollipop taped to it. He made sure yours stood out."

The memory hits me: the fluorescent lights of the classroom, James standing there, holding that Valentine with his crooked grin. The card wasn't anything fancy — just a simple heart cut out of red construction paper with a Tootsie Pop taped to the front.

"I remember going home that day," Donnie continues. "And I was so mad. At James. At you. At the whole damn thing."

I look at him, confused. "Why?"

"Because I saw the way he looked at you, Betty. He's *always* looked at you like that... like you're the only person in the room." He hesitates. "I was a kid... but I knew, even then, that James Cohen would never look at me that way."

I stare at him, my throat tightening. This isn't about prom. This isn't about a cherry lollipop. This isn't even about me. It's just Donnie — awkward, honest, and asking me to prom. Like it's that simple.

So I say yes.

Not to make a point. Not to pity Donnie. Not because it

makes the ache go away. But because for once, I don't want to be the girl waiting around to be chosen. This time, I want to choose. Myself.

"James kissed me over winter break," I mutter quietly.

Donnie looks up, surprised.

"Then acted like it never happened."

Donnie's face shifts, just slightly. But he doesn't push. Doesn't ask for more. He just gives me this quiet, understanding nod.

"I'm glad you said yes," he says after a while.

"I'm glad you asked." And I mean it.

Chapter 42
The Middle Seat
Donnie

I walk the two blocks home, cutting through the church parking lot because I like the irony. The Pilgrims — good, God-fearing folk who attend Sunday service in ironed khakis and polos.

When I round the corner near the playground, I slip on my headphones and hit play on my Discman. *My Sharona* starts playing — loud and definitely banned in the Pilgrim household. Mom says the lyrics "poison the mind," like they're some sort of gateway drug.

Which, honestly, only makes me like it more.

By the time I reach the porch, I can already smell the smoke. Mom's burning the chicken and humming along to a cassette labeled *Heavenly Gospel Hymns Vol. III*.

"Hey, honey," Mom chirps. "How was school?"

"I got a prom date."

Her eyebrows lift, like she just witnessed a miracle. "Oh, that's wonderful! Who's the lucky girl?"

I almost don't want to tell her.

It'll be the hot topic of discussion in the Pilgrim household at Easter and probably through Thanksgiving. Because — *shocker* — Donnie Pilgrim managed to convince a girl to go to prom with him.

There'll be teasing from my little sister, raised eyebrows from the aunts, Grandma will probably ask if she's Methodist, Dad will ask when the wedding is, and my older brother will just be glad that a girl finally glanced my way.

But none of them will ask me how it felt to hear her say yes. And I wouldn't know how to answer even if they did.

I hesitate, then sigh. "Betty."

"That red-haired girl?" She pauses. "She's... nice."

Translation: I went to her grandmother's cookie exchange and not a single nativity in sight — just too many bottles of merlot and Nat King Cole singing about chestnuts as if *that's* what Christmas is about.

She turns back to the stove, whisking the mashed potatoes like her life depends on it. "Isn't she dating that Cohen boy?"

I shrug.

Mom smiles, a little wistfully. "James was always such a sweet boy. I remember when he climbed the monkey bars so you wouldn't be scared to try them alone."

"Well, I'm off to braid him a friendship bracelet," I say before disappearing into my room.

The wallpaper in my room is baby blue and dotted with tiny sailboats. A leftover relic from when I was seven and thought I'd grow up to be a sea captain.

Now I'm seventeen. And just trying not to drown.

I lie on my bed and stare at the ceiling. It's cracked in one corner, like everything else around here. I should feel happy. I have a date for prom. I'm not a total loser.

So why do I feel so empty inside?

At school the next day, I do what I do best — blend in. People talk about prom and tux rentals and who's booking a limo. I nod at all the right moments. Laugh when I'm supposed to. But I still feel like an outcast.

I catch a glimpse of Miles in the hallway between third and fourth period. He's leaning against a locker, laughing at something too hard. I walk the long way around to avoid him.

And then, I spot James by the vending machines. He's kicking one like it personally insulted him. Slouched shoulders. Messy hair. Hands shoved into the pockets of his denim jacket. Classic James Cohen.

"Try sweet-talking it," I say, coming up beside him. "I hear they respond well to compliments."

He smirks, looking at me. The bruise under his eye is still there. Finally, a Dr. Pepper drops into the tray.

"Guess that sweet-talking trick works," James says, reaching down to grab the can.

"You gonna have that shiner for prom?" I ask, nodding toward his face.

He touches it instinctively. "It looked worse a few days ago." Then he adds, more quietly, "Thanks. For getting Mr. Harrison at camp. It might've ended a lot worse if you hadn't."

I shrug. "Don't mention it."

He pops the can open and takes a swig. "So, who are you taking to prom?"

"Betty."

He looks at me. And for a moment, he looks angry, like he wants to hit me. But I know he won't.

Instead, he just nods, saying, "Good. She deserves a nice night."

"Yeah." I feel something tightening in my chest. "She does."

He nods again, like he doesn't know what else to say. Like he's not entirely sure what this means. For her. For me. For him. But we don't talk about that.

"James, can I ask you something?"

"Sure, shoot."

"Why did you start that fight with Miles?"

James stiffens. Instantly.

I push on. "I overheard some of what was said. I know it had to do with Betty. And whatever it is... it's been eating at you."

James doesn't answer at first.

"Something —" He shifts on his feet, jaw clenched. "Something really bad happened. At Nina's party."

The bell rings.

"Shit," he mutters. "I'm gonna be late for chem." He pats my shoulder and jogs toward the stairwell. Then, he stops.

"Donnie," he says, looking over his shoulder. "You're a good friend."

For a second, I let myself believe he might mean it. I watch him go, thinking not for the first time... it's never going to be me.

After school, I get stuck in the middle seat of Mom's Buick, wedged between my little sister's flute case and a Tupperware full of deviled eggs for Youth Group. My sister refuses to sit in the back because she swears she gets car sick if she's not sitting shotgun.

I know that's bullshit. But she's twelve. And the youngest. And the only daughter. Meanwhile, I'm five-foot-eleven, but hey, that doesn't matter in my family.

Middle child. Middle seat.

At home, I lie on my bed again. Same ceiling. Same baby blue wallpaper. I think about prom. About Betty. And then I remember the look on her face when she said yes. Not pitying. Not confused. Just... soft. Like she saw something in me that I don't even see in myself.

I want to hold onto that. Because I might not get the fairytale ending. I might not ever say what I really want to say. But for one night, I get to be the boy who takes the girl to prom. And maybe that's enough. At least for now.

Chapter 43
The Cave
Betty

The storm clouds loom overhead as I make my way through the forest, the sound of my footsteps muffled by the soft carpet of pine needles beneath my shoes. I take a seat on the grassy bank, pulling my knees to my chest and resting my chin on them. The creek moves slowly today, so slow that I'm able to watch tiny tadpoles dart through the water.

Then I hear footsteps.

"Dorothea said I might find you here," James says, settling beside me.

"This used to be our place," I say, glancing at him. "Did you ever bring—"

"No, never," James interjects. "This is still our place." He looks at me. "It will always be our place."

A weird feeling settles in the pit of my stomach hearing that — a comforting feeling.

"You said you were looking for me?" I calmly remind him.

I can feel my heart beating a little faster, my mind racing with all the possibilities of what he might say next.

"We just... I don't know." He's quiet for a second. "I guess, I just... I needed to see you."

I look away, poking a stick into the mud to avoid his gaze.

"Well, here I am."

"There you are."

My eyes flicker to James's face, and I notice it: the purple bruise beneath his left eye.

"What happened to your eye?"

His gaze drops for a moment before locking with mine again. "It's nothing."

"Does it hurt?" I ask, leaning closer.

"I'm fine." His eyes snap away. "Donnie told me that you're going to prom with him," he adds, his voice tightening. "Is that true?"

"Yeah, I am."

His jaw clenches. "So are you guys a thing now?"

"Why does it matter to you?" I shoot back, raising an eyebrow.

He sighs, shaking his head. "Just tell me, are you?"

"No, it's not like that," I reply. "We're friends."

The sky begins to darken, and the gentle murmur of the creek is drowned out by the rumble of thunder.

"We'd better head back," James says, looking up at the clouds. "Looks like it's going to be a pretty bad storm."

I stand, feeling James's gaze burning into my back.

As we trek down the dirt path, the rain begins to fall in heavy sheets. I glance back at James, his figure blurred by the downpour.

"Come on, I know where we can take shelter!" he calls.

As we scramble through the undergrowth, lightning flashes in the distance, illuminating the path ahead. Finally, we stumble upon a small cave nestled beneath the canopy of trees. We huddle inside, our wet bodies pressed together as we catch our breath.

The storm howls outside, wind curling through the cave's narrow mouth like it's trying to drag us back out. My clothes cling to my skin, but it's not the cold making me shiver.

It's everything we're not saying.

"You know what's funny?" I finally say, shaking my head. "I've spent so long waiting for you. And now that you're finally here... it's not because you chose me."

James frowns. "What are you talking about?"

"You kissed me, James." My voice cracks. "That night in the turret. You kissed me. Like I was everything. Then left me like I was nothing."

His face pales, a raindrop trailing down the tip of his nose

"I mean, what was that? A mistake? A joke?" I hug my knees to my chest. "Was it one last taste to help you decide if you really are in love with her?"

James stiffens. "It's not that simple."

"Explain it to me then!" I snap. "Because I've been going crazy trying to figure it out. You say you miss me. You drop everything when I need you. You *kiss* me. Then you disappear for months and go back to her. Every. Single. Time."

"I-I don't know." James scrubs a hand down his face, frustrated. "I guess I thought that walking away from her after everything would make me a terrible person." He swallows, voice softer now. "And after Homecoming... after what happened between Cassie and me, I—" His eyes flick away from mine.

"What?" I narrow my eyes. "What happened between you two?"

He suddenly looks like he wants to be anywhere else but in this cave with me.

"You slept with her." The words fall out before I can stop them. "Oh my god, you slept with her... didn't you?"

He doesn't deny it.

My stomach drops. I turn away from him, something inside me splintering.

"Betty, wait—"

I don't let him finish. I walk out of the cave, out into the cold, steady drizzle. The rain soaks through my clothes, chills my skin, but I barely feel it. I hear James running behind me and turn to face him.

"You can't tell me that kiss didn't mean anything." I blink the rain from my lashes, my voice trembling. "You can't look me in the eyes and say it wasn't real."

"Of course it was real, Betty."

"Then why did you leave me?" I scoff, voice shaking. "Why

did you leave me that night — in the turret?"

"I-I panicked." James exhales, running a hand through his hair. "I was scared. Scared of hurting Cassie. Scared of screwing things up with you again." He stops, closing his eyes like he's trying to block the memory from resurfacing. "I'm sorry, I never meant to hurt you."

"But you did hurt me." I wipe the water from my cheeks, though I'm not sure how much of it is rain and how much is tears.

He looks at me, guilt flashing in his eyes. His clothes are soaked, hair dripping, but he doesn't move. Suddenly, I don't see the boy I've loved since I was four. I see someone who is just as broken and confused as I am.

James glances at the sky, where patches of blue peek out through the dissipating clouds, and for a moment, I think he's going to leave, walk away without ever speaking to me again. But instead, he reaches out to me, his eyes softening.

We stumble along the path together, wet and muddy, taking in the destruction left by the storm. The low-hanging branch that once held our rope swing has snapped off and now lies in the creek.

A frog hops onto a log in front of me. He's small, with a brown speckled back, just sitting there, blinking. I watch it for a moment, and then it hops away, back into the underbrush.

Chapter 44
Cracks
Cassie

I concentrate on not tripping over the hem of my dress, but the fabric catches on my heels every time I move too quickly. I pause, glancing over my shoulder. Betty's on the dance floor, spinning with Donnie. She's laughing — and for a second, I smile. It's nice to see her happy.

But then, out of the corner of my eye, I see Miles lurking in the shadows like a predator. My stomach knots. Something about the way he's looking at her makes my skin crawl. I pick up my pace, focusing only on Betty. I'm trying not to panic, trying not to imagine what he's thinking — what he's planning.

I'm just a few steps away from Betty when—

"Hey, Parker."

"What do you want?" I glare at him, my pulse quickening.

"Jesus, can't a guy say hello?" Miles leans in, his voice a low, sinister whisper. "But since you asked, I just want you to know that your golden boy James isn't as golden as he seems."

I shake my head, trying to brush past him, but he grabs my arm with an iron-like hold. I try to yank my arm away, but his bony fingers tighten around my wrist.

"Let me finish," he murmurs, his breath warm against my ear. "Did you know he's the reason I got suspended for a week? Almost missed prom because of him."

"How unfortunate," I say, my voice flat. "I wish you did."

"Sorry to disappoint." Miles' eyes gleam. He tilts his head, savoring every word. "Did you know he kissed Betty?"

I freeze, glancing over at James. He's walking through the crowd, two cups of punch in his hands like nothing's wrong. I catch a glimpse of Betty. She's frozen mid-spin, her gaze flicking to me.

"You're lying," I say, trembling at the edges.

Miles clicks his tongue, almost pitying. "You're so naive. It's almost cute." He leans in closer. "Ask him yourself."

Without thinking, I turn on my heel and bolt from the gym. I don't even know where I'm running. I just know I have to *go*. Somewhere. Anywhere. Away from all of it — from the lights, the music, the lies.

I push through the main doors. Behind me, James's voice cuts through the haze. Sharp. Desperate. I hear him call my name — once, then again.

"Cassie — stop!"

I don't stop.

Not until I feel his hand catch my arm. But I can't bear the thought of his touch. Not right now. I yank my arm free and turn to face him.

"Did you kiss Betty?"

James's face twists. "Wh—who told you that?"

"Just answer me."

"Cassie, please, let me explain—"

"Oh my god." It slips out in a whisper, more to myself than to him. "So it's true." I shake my head, a bitter laugh bubbling up, catching in my throat. "Of course it's true."

"It didn't mean anything," he says quickly. "The kiss—it didn't mean anything. I swear."

Even in the dark, I can see the cracks in his face, in his voice. The truth is spilling out, whether he means it to or not.

I meet his eyes.

"You and I both know that's not true." My voice trembles, but I don't stop. "You've loved Betty since the moment she came back. Quite frankly, I don't think you ever stopped." I push on. "And I hope you don't think I'm so stupid that I didn't see it. I did. The whole time." My throat tightens. "I just didn't want to believe it."

"I'm sorry, Cassie. I never wanted to hurt you. I swear."

I nod. He didn't hurt me out of cruelty or malice. It wasn't intentional. It wasn't evil — just confusion. Just carelessness. He's an eighteen-year-old boy.

"I don't regret it," I say softly, "I'm grateful I got to know, even for a little while, what it feels like to be loved by James Cohen."

I hold his gaze, just for a second longer. Then I walk away, leaving behind the boy who shattered my heart and the remnants of a love that was never truly mine.

Chapter 45
Second Choice
James

I push through the doors to the gymnasium, my eyes darting around the room of slow dancers. I spot Betty across the gym, in that periwinkle dress, laughing at something Donnie just said.

Cassie dumped me. I should feel wrecked. I do feel wrecked. But mostly, I feel hollow. Like I've just stepped off a cliff and realized I forgot my parachute halfway down. And now Betty's standing right there. What if I've already ruined everything? What if it's too late?

Still, I have to try, right? I have to know if there's still something between us. If the part of her that used to love me still exists. And if I get this wrong, if she looks at me like I'm just another mistake, then maybe I deserve that, too.

I take a deep breath and amble over to her.

"Hey," I say, trying to sound casual despite the nerves fluttering in my stomach. "Mind if I steal a dance with her?"

Betty shoots a glance at Donnie, silently asking for his approval. His grin widens into a nod. And in response, she offers a gentle nod of her own.

"Where's Cassie?" Betty says, wrapping her hands around my shoulders.

"She left," I admit, trying to keep my voice steady.

"I'm sorry," she says, but it sounds more like disappointment than comfort.

The music hums around us. I can smell her perfume — the same scent from the turret that night. I study her face, every freckle, every flicker of hesitation in her eyes. She's beautiful. Standing this close to her again, it's like nothing's changed. But everything *has*.

"Betty, I—"

Then suddenly, I don't think. I reach down, gently cupping her cheeks, tilting her face toward mine. She pulls away, her soft expression hardening into a steely glare.

"James, stop."

"Betty, come on," I say, grabbing her hands. "We can be together again."

"Are you hearing yourself right now?" She shakes her head, backing away. "You think everything can magically reset to the way things used to be? Like it suddenly erases everything that's happened?"

"Betty, no... I—"

"I can't. Not like this." She takes a step back. "I refuse to be anyone's second choice. I hate that feeling. I want you to fight for me, to choose me, and not just when it's convenient for you." And with that, she turns and walks away.

Suddenly, I feel a hand clamp onto my shoulder. Turning, I meet Donnie's gaze.

"Donnie," I start, but he cuts me off.

"Jesus, James," he says flatly. "Are you seriously that dense?"

"Look, I didn't—" I stammer, still trying to process everything. "I thought she'd understand."

Donnie rolls his eyes, exasperated. "Understand what, exactly?" he shoots back. "That after stringing her along all year, you can just waltz back and expect her to swoon over you?"

I don't have a defense. Not a good one, anyway.

"She's been waiting on you, man." He shakes his head, almost pitying me. "Waiting for you to figure your shit out while you bounced between two girls and hurt *both* of them."

"How did you know—"

"How did I know? Dude, everyone saw you chase Cassie outside. Then we all heard Betty chew your ass out. It doesn't take a rocket scientist to figure out."

My throat tightens. He's not wrong.

"Betty deserves more than some half-assed confession just because things didn't work out with Cassie." Donnie takes a step back, letting out a breath. "If you care about Betty, then show it. But stop playing with her feelings."

The sting of his words settles in, and I finally nod.

He watches me for a second, then his tone softens. "I'm gonna go find my prom date and take her home." His eyes flick past me toward the dance floor.

I stand there, feeling like an idiot. I thought choosing Betty would fix everything. But maybe that's the problem — I still thought this was about choosing.

Chapter 46
The Most Venomous Snakes are Green
Betty

I grip the edge of the bathroom sink, staring at my reflection in the dim, flickering light. Mascara smudges beneath my eyes. I grab a paper towel and wipe at my cheeks, scrubbing away the remnants of my tears, as if I can erase the hurt along with it. My hands tremble, but I force myself to breathe.

With one last glance in the mirror, I square my shoulders, lift my chin, and walk out of the bathroom. I refuse to be the girl who crumbles. Not tonight. Not ever again.

But then, I hear Miles. His voice slithers through the corridor, sharp and venomous, punctuated by a few hushed snickers from others. My stomach tightens as I round the corner and see him leaning against the wall, cornering Donnie.

"I don't understand how this faggot managed to get a date."

My blood goes cold.

"What... did you have to pay her or something?"

Donnie tightens his jaw, pushing his glasses up with quivering fingers. I see it in his posture — the same smallness I used to feel when Carrigan snickered my name like I was less than human.

"Come on, how much did you pay her?" Miles sneers, but before he can say another word, I step in front of Donnie.

Miles tilts his head, smirking. "The hell are you doing, Thompson?"

"You don't get to stand here and treat people like this." My voice is low, sharp. "Not anymore."

Miles stiffens, but he doesn't say a word.

I take a step closer, so close I can see the exact shade of his irises.

"I was seven years old when my mom warned me that some of the most venomous snakes are green." I tilt my head, giving him a look that's almost pitying. "And I was seventeen when I looked into your green eyes and realized how right she was."

Miles's smirk falters for half a second. Just a flicker. But I see it, and that's all I need. I grab Donnie's arm and pull him past Miles, past the lingering group of guys, past the remnants of something I refuse to let define me anymore.

The moment we're outside, Donnie exhales sharply. "Holy shit, Betty."

I glance at him with a small, knowing grin. "He's not going to bother us anymore."

And with that, we leave Miles where he belongs.

In the past.

Chapter 47
Be Here

James

The principal drones through the names. Applause erupts, dies down, erupts again. I didn't expect high school graduation to be *this* boring.

Somewhere in the sea of caps, I see her. Three rows ahead. She doesn't look back. It's like I'm invisible. Or worse, like I don't exist anymore.

They call Betty's name before mine. I watch her climb the stairs, her shoulders straight, her robe a little too big. Mom probably would've cried. She always had a soft spot for Betty — always hoped we'd end up together one day.

After the ceremony ends, I weave through the crowd toward the parking lot. Dad's leaning against the hood of my truck, arms crossed. The afternoon sun catches the silver in his hair. He looks tired. Not angry. Just worn out.

My chest tightens — not from nerves, but from the weight of everything that's gone unsaid between us. Especially since the night I got sent home from Kanawha. I was pacing the living room, fists clenched, trying to make him understand.

"I wasn't just fighting for no reason, Dad. The other guy, Miles, he—"

"I don't want to hear another excuse." He didn't even look up. Just kept sorting his paperwork. "You've got to learn to

walk away from these things."

"Easy for you to say. You left us after Mom died."

That's when his eyes snapped up. Cold. Defensive.

"Don't bring your mother into this."

"Why not? You think working long hours and paying the bills makes up for the fact that you're never home? You think that's enough? Julie and I needed you. We still do."

Something in him shifted then. Softened.

He ran a hand through his graying hair, his voice quieter. "I know I haven't been perfect. I just... I miss her, James."

"You don't have to fix it all, Dad. Just... be here."

Now, I see my father not as the distant man I once made him out to be, but as a man burdened by his regrets and grief.

He looks at me and places a firm hand on my shoulder. "Congratulations, James. I am proud of you."

Before I can stop myself, I step forward and pull him into a hug. He's stiff at first, like he doesn't know what to do. But then he squeezes back — and for the first time in six years, it feels like I have my dad again.

I meet Julie at Marg's later that evening — the first time seeing her since she finished her spring semester at Ohio University. She slides into the booth across from me, still in her campus hoodie, messy hair piled on top of her head.

She looks at me. "So, I decided what I want to do."

"Yeah?" I lean in.

"I want to be a high school teacher."

"Like Mom," I say quietly, nodding.

Julie nods too. "Like Mom."

I smile. "That's great, Jules. I'm happy for you."

"And James," Julie cuts into her cherry pie. "I saw the way you looked at Betty during the ceremony. What's going on with you two?"

I sigh. "I think she's done with me. For good this time."

Julie tilts her head slightly, studying me, and then shoves a forkful of pie in her mouth.

"I tried talking to her at prom." I pick at the edge of my napkin. "Yeah... it didn't go so well."

"I heard that you professed your love for her minutes after things ended with Cassie," Julie scoffs, stabbing her pie.

"How did you even find out about that?"

"I have my connections."

I lean back in my seat with a sigh.

"Be the guy she thought you were, James. The one *she* knew. Not the clueless idiot who couldn't make up his mind."

"What if she slams the door in my face?"

Julie shrugs. "Then at least you'll know you tried." She slides her car keys across the table. "Just go."

Chapter 48
Here's to Karma, Baby

Betty

The diploma is warm in my hands, like it just came off the printer. It's lighter than I imagined. I always thought it would feel heavier, like it should carry the weight of every tear, heartbreak, and burst of laughter that led to this moment.

I look up, and then I see him.

"Dad?"

I didn't expect him to come, but there he is, standing between Mom and Grandma, his gaze locked on me.

"Hey, squirt," he says, approaching.

I swallow hard, feeling a lump in my throat. "I... I didn't think you'd come."

"Why in the world would you think that?" He steps closer, reaching out to place a hand on my shoulder. "You think I wouldn't come to my only daughter's high school graduation?"

Tears well up in my eyes.

"I wouldn't miss this day for the world." He pulls me into a hug, holding me tight.

As I break away, I see Mom, her eyes glistening with tears. "You've grown into such a strong and beautiful woman." She holds me at arm's length, brushing a stray tear from my cheek.

I turn to Grandma, standing just behind them, her eyes a little misty. She opens her arms without a word, and I melt into them like I'm seven again, safe from everything.

"I always knew you'd shine," she whispers. "You just had to come home first."

As I wipe my eyes, blinking away the last of the tears, I catch a glimpse of Donnie. He's standing off to the side, looking out over the crowd with that slightly awkward stance. The sunlight glints off his glasses, and for a second, I just watch him.

We've come a long way, and even though this day is supposed to be about moving forward, I feel this strange pull to make sure nothing is left unsaid between us.

"Donnie," I call, weaving through the crowd toward him.

He turns, a smile beaming across his face. "We made it — kinda feels surreal, doesn't it? But hey, at least I can finally stop pretending to pay attention to Mr. Hair's riveting lectures."

"Or dodging gym class."

He laughs, then shifts his weight. "Oh, guess what?" he says, a sly grin stretching across his face. "I heard Miles lost his scholarship to Johns Hopkins."

I blink. "Are you serious?"

Donnie nods, looking downright giddy. "Guess being a raging asshole finally caught up to him."

"Holy shit." I let out a disbelieving snort. "Karma finally did her job?"

"Took her long enough." He bumps his shoulder into mine.

For a moment, we just stand there. There's a comfortable silence between us now, something that didn't exist before.

He reaches into his bag and pulls out his yearbook. "I think signing these things are pretty stupid, frankly because I don't give a damn about this place, but what the hell." He holds it out. "Betty, will you sign mine?"

"I'd be honored."

I try to think of something witty. Or heartfelt. Or maybe words of encouragement. Instead, I take the purple gel pen and write in big, bold letters —

HERE'S TO KARMA, BABY

He reads it and smiles — not the big, mischievous grin he saves for mouthing off in class, but something softer. Realer.

Then he closes the yearbook and says, "I'm keeping this. For when you win a Pulitzer Prize. That way, I can brag I got your autograph before the rest of the world caught on."

"Keep dreaming, Pilgrim." I smile, shaking my head.

He takes a step back, holding his diploma up. "Now," he says, grinning. "Let's get the hell out of Ohio."

I think about what comes next — all the unknowns, all the fear. But standing here with Donnie, it doesn't feel so scary anymore.

Chapter 49
Speckled Brown Frog
James

I knock three times, my hand slick with sweat. When the door opens, she's there — in an oversized t-shirt, hair twisted into two messy braids. I can't tell if she's happy to see me or if she's about to slam the door in my face.

"James?" Betty steps out, closing the door behind her.

"I made this for you," I say, holding out a mixed tape. "I'm sorry. I was an idiot at prom — I hurt you. And I'll regret that for a long time."

She takes the mixtape with a slight smile.

I take a step forward, closing the gap between us. "I love you, Betty," I say, heart pounding. "Like madly, out-of-my-mind in love with you."

"Do you know how many nights I cried myself to sleep, wishing you'd say those words to me?" she says, shaking her head. "And now, after everything. After prom. After Cassie. *Now* you say them?"

"I know." I sigh. "I should've said it sooner. I should've said it that night in the turret and a hundred times before that. I should've never made you doubt it for a second."

"And you think showing up with a mixed tape fixes everything?"

"No," I admit. "But it's a start. And I'd show up a thousand more times if it meant getting one more chance with you."

She's quiet for a moment, but something in her expression shifts—still guarded, but softer now. Her arms wrap around herself like she's holding something in.

"I'm going to Cornell University," she says finally, her lips curving into a small, tentative smile. "To study English Literature."

I blink. "Betty, that's incredible."

"I leave next month," she says. "I got accepted into a writing seminar for incoming freshmen." She pauses, eyes flicking down to the ground before lifting to meet mine again. "I think it's time for me to release the tadpoles in my jar."

"What do you mean?"

"It's like when we were kids," she begins. "They're everything I've carried with me— memories, feelings, all the stuff I could never let go of. But if I release them back into the creek, the tadpoles are free to swim. And so can I."

I stare at her, and for a second, I don't even know what to say.

"Well," I say finally, rubbing the back of my neck with a faint smile, "looks like we're both heading to New York, then. My acceptance letter to NYU came last week."

She raises an eyebrow in surprise, then smiles. "There's a train from Ithaca to New York City."

She says it like a fact, like she's already memorized the

train schedule. But when I meet her eyes, I realize it's not just about the train. It's about us.

Without a word, she steps forward, wrapping her arms around me in an embrace. The last time she hugged me like this was the day she left for New York, her face buried in my chest, her fingers trembling, both of us scared. That hug felt like goodbye. Like the unraveling of something.

But this one feels different. It feels like hope.

New beginnings.

Chapter 50
One Year Later
Betty

Cassie cut her hair to her shoulders since I last saw her. She tells me her dad finally came around, and they are patching things up slowly. Her mom still doesn't talk to her. But Cassie says it doesn't ache as much as it used to.

I didn't plan on becoming friends with Cassie — it just sort of happened. It began the day I was packing up Mom's car to leave for Ithaca. Cassie had stopped by the house, and to be honest, I half-expected her to tell me to go to hell.

But that's not Cassie.

Instead, she brought up that night at camp and how much she missed having someone to talk to. Annoyingly, I realized I felt the same way. After we finished loading up the car, we decided to grab a bite at Marg's. We had cherry pie and hot chocolate, and somehow, despite everything, we just clicked.

In a way, we're sort of kindred spirits. Funny how life works like that. A year ago, I wouldn't have imagined us standing together in McGregor's Nook, flipping through stacks of dusty books together.

But here we are.

"Betty, you should read this one," Cassie says, handing me a book with a knowing smile. "I think you'll love it."

I take the book from her, admiring its intricate cover.

"I've been meaning to tell you," Cassie begins lightly. "I'm taking a gap year."

"A gap year?" I say, surprised. "But what about Yale?"

"It's one of the oldest schools in the country." Cassie smiles. "It'll still be there."

"What will you do?"

"I'm going to teach ballet. At a little studio just around the corner." She tilts her head. "I want to spend a year figuring out who I am. Learning to love myself again."

I nod, watching the way the light catches the dust floating in the air between us. "I think that's wonderful, Cassie."

She smiles again. "I think it's overdue."

Mr. McGregor approaches with a teapot shaped like a cat.

"Here you go, girls!" he announces cheerfully, placing it on a nearby table. Then with a wink, he says, "Betty, go have a look behind the register."

So I do.

Hanging on the wall, slightly faded, is one of my poems — the one I scribbled in blue ink on a napkin and tucked into a copy of *The Bell Jar* like a secret.

It wasn't the best thing I'd ever written. But Mr. McGregor kept it. Framed it. And hung it in his bookstore.

As the afternoon drifts by, the sunlight slowly begins to shift. Before we part ways, Cassie and I exchange hugs with promises to keep in touch. I steal one last glance at Mr.

McGregor, who watches us with a warm smile.

Stepping outside, my eyes immediately find James. He turns, his face lighting up with that familiar, crooked smile. James fell in love with the city during his first year at NYU. I rode the train back and forth to him so many times that the conductors started setting aside a cherry Coke and a pack of peanut M&Ms for me.

"So, what's the plan?" I ask, slipping my hand into his.

"How about Coney Island?"

We stroll along the boardwalk, gazing at the ocean view. As the sun begins to set, we find a quiet spot on the beach.

"I've been working on something," I begin, my fingers raking through the sand. "A short story. About a girl. A boy. And a creek." I glance at him. "Want to hear it?"

He nods, the ocean breeze tousling his hair.

I pull a folded notebook page from my bag, smoothing it over my knees.

Then I begin to read:

"The summer I turned seven, James and I discovered the magic of the creek. We ran barefoot down the dirt path, wildflowers and tall grass brushing against our ankles. The trail was lined with monstrous trees, their branches stretched out as if they might reach down and grab us. When we arrived, we dipped our toes into the cool, rippling water — and everything else seemingly faded away."

His face stills, then breaks into a soft smile — the kind that belongs to someone who remembers.

Every word.

Every jar. Every tadpole.

Every splash of muddy water between us.

And as we sit here, the tide lapping at our toes, I've come to understand that it was never our creek in Gallipolis that brought us together — it was something deeper. Something that's always been there.

And because of that, I kept one tadpole. He grew into a frog with bent legs and a speckled brown back — not perfect, but still beautiful. Because no matter where life takes me, a piece of my heart will always belong to the boy from across the street.

About the Author

Mary Kathryn Groh is a writer based in Cincinnati, Ohio. A lifelong lover of storytelling, she grew up filling notebooks with journal entries and made-up worlds as her favorite creative escape. When she's not writing, she's usually sipping coffee, rewatching her comfort shows, or cuddling with her orange cat, Ruby.

Tadpoles in My Jar is her debut novel, and it's a love letter to small towns, nostalgia, coming-of-age summers, and the people who shape us during the most pivotal moments of our lives.